The Camberwell Beauty
and Other Stories

V. S. Pritchett

The Camberwell Beauty

and Other Stories

RANDOM HOUSE · NEW YORK

Copyright © 1974 by Victor S. Pritchett

All rights reserved under International and Pan-American Copyright Conventions. Published in the United States by Random House, Inc., New York.

Library of Congress Cataloging in Publication Data

Pritchett, Victor Sawdon, 1900–
    The Camberwell beauty, and other stories.

    CONTENTS: The Camberwell beauty.—The marvellous girl—The lady from Guatemala.   [etc.]
    I.   Title.
PZ3.P9395Cam3   [PS6031.R7]   823'.9'12   74–5215
ISBN 0–49222–6

"The Diver," originally entitled "The Fall," and "Our Wife," originally entitled "The Captain's Daughter," first appeared in *The New Yorker*. Copyright © 1969 by V. S. Pritchett.
"Marvellous Girl" and "The Rescue" originally appeared in *The New Yorker*. Copyright © 1973 by V. S. Pritchett.
"Lady from Guatemala," "Did You Invite Me?" and "The Spree" originally appeared in *Playboy*. Copyright © 1974 by V. S. Pritchett.
"The Last Throw" originally appeared in *Encounter*. Copyright © 1974 by V. S. Pritchett.

Manufactured in the United States of America

98765432

First Edition

To my wife

Contents

The Camberwell Beauty

August's? On the Bath road? Twice-Five August—of course I knew August: ivory man. And the woman who lived with him—her name was Price. She's dead. He went out of business years ago. He's probably dead too. I was in the trade only three or four years but I soon knew every antique dealer in the South of England. I used to go to all the sales. Name another. Naseley of Close Place? Jades, Asiatics, never touched India; Alsop of Ramsey? Ephemera. Marbright, High Street, Boxley? Georgian silver. Fox? Are you referring to Fox of Denton or Fox of Camden —William Morris, art nouveau—or the Fox Brothers in the Portobello Road?—the eldest stuttered. They had an uncle in Brighton who went mad looking for old Waterford. Hindmith? No, he was just a copier. Ah now, Pliny! He was a very different cup of tea: Caughley ware. (Coalport took it over in 1821.) I am speaking of specialties: furniture is the bread and butter of the trade. It keeps a man going while his mind is on his specialty and within that specialty there is one object he broods on from one year to the next, most of his life: the thing a man would commit murder to get his hands on if he had the nerve, but I have never heard of a dealer who had. Theft perhaps. A stagnant lot. But if he does get hold of that thing he will never let it go or certainly not to a customer—

dealers only really like dealing among themselves—but every other dealer in the trade knows he's got it. So they sit in their shops reading the catalogs and watching one another. Fox broods on something Alsop has. Alsop has his eye on Pliny and Pliny puts his hands to one of his big red ears when he hears the name of August. At the heart of the trade is lust, but a lust that is a dream paralyzed by itself. So paralyzed that the only release, the only hope, as everyone knows, is disaster: a bankruptcy, a divorce, a court case, a burglary, trouble with the police, a death. Perhaps then the grip on some piece of treasure will weaken and fall into the watcher's hands and even if it goes elsewhere he will go on dreaming about it.

What was it that Pliny, Gentleman Pliny, wanted of a man like August who was not much better than a country junk dealer? When I opened up in London I thought it was a particular Staffordshire figure, but Pliny was far above that. These figures fetch very little, though one or two are hard to find: "The Burning of Cranmer," for example. Very few were made; it never sold and the firm dropped it. I was young and eager and one day when a collector, a scholarly man, as dry as a stick, came to my shop and told me he had a complete collection except for this piece, I said in my innocent way: "You've come to the right man. I'm fairly certain I can get it for you—at a price." This was a lie; but I was astonished to see the old man look at me with contempt, then light up like a fire, and when he left, look back furtively at me: he had betrayed his lust.

You rarely see an antique shop standing on its own; there are always three or four together watching each other. I asked the advice of the man next door who ran a small boatyard on the canal in his spare time and he said, "Try Pliny down the Green: he knows everyone." I went "over the water," to Pliny; he was closed, but I did find him at last at a sale room. Pliny was marking his catalog and waiting for the next lot to come up and he said to me in a scornful way, slapping a young man down, "August's got it." I saw him wink at the man next to him as I left.

I had bought myself a small red car that annoyed the older dealers and I drove down the other side of Steepleton on the Bath road. August's was one of four shops opposite the Lion Hotel on the main road at the end of the town where the country begins again, and there I got my first lesson. The shop was closed. I went across to the bar of the hotel, and August was there, a fat man of fifty in wide trousers and a drip to his nose who was paying for drinks from a bunch of dirty notes in his jacket pocket and dropping them on the floor. He was drunk and very offended when I picked a couple up and gave them to him. He'd just come back from Newbury races. I humored him but he kept rolling about and turning his back to me half the time and so I blurted out, "I've just been over at the shop. You've got some Staffordshire I hear."

He stood still and looked me up and down and the beer swelled in him.

"Who may you be?" he said with all the pomposity of drink. I told him. I said right out, "Staffordshire. 'Cranmer's Burning.'" His face went dead and the color of liver.

"So is London," he said and turned away to the bar.

"I'm told you might have it. I've got a collector," I said.

"Give this lad a glass of water," said August to the barmaid. "He's on fire."

There is nothing more to say about the evening or the many other visits I made to August's except that it has a moral to it and that I had to help August over to his shop, where an enormous woman much taller than he in a black dress and a little girl of fourteen or so were at the

door waiting for him. The girl looked frightened and ran
a few yards from the door as August and his woman
collided belly to belly.

"Come back," called the woman.

The child crept back. And to me the woman said,
"We're closed," and having got the two inside, shut the
door in my face.

The moral is this: if "The Burning of Cranmer" was
August's treasure, it was hopeless to try and get it before
he had time to guess what mine was. It was clear to him
I was too new to the trade to have one. And, in fact, I
don't think he had the piece. Years later, I found my
collector had left his collection complete to a private
museum in Leicester when he died. He had obtained
what he craved: a small immortality in being memorable
for his relation to a minor work of art.

I know what happened at August's that night. In time,
his woman, Mrs. Price, bellowed it to me, for her confi-
dences could be heard down the street. August flopped
on his bed, and while he was sleeping off the drink she
got the bundles of notes out of his pockets and counted
them. She always did this after his racing days. If he had
lost she woke him up and shouted at him; if he had made
a profit she kept quiet and hid it under her clothes in a
chest of drawers. I went down from London again and
again, but August was not there.

Most of the time these shops are closed. You rattle the
door handle; no reply. Look through the window, and
each object inside stands gleaming with something like
a smile of malice, especially on porcelain and glass. The
furniture states placidly that it has been in better houses
than you will ever have, the brass speaks of vanished
servants. Everything speaks of the dead hands that have
touched it; even the dust is like the dust of vanished
families. In the shabby places—and August's was shabby
—the dealer is like a toadstool that has grown out of the

unwanted. There was only one attractive object in August's shop—as I say, he went in for ivories and on a table at the back was a set of white and red chessmen set out on a board partly concealed by a screen. I was tapping my feet impatiently and looking through the window when I was astonished to see two of the chessmen had moved; then I saw a hand, a long, thin work-reddened hand appear from behind the screen and move one of the pieces back. Life in the place! I rattled the door handle again and the child came from behind the screen. She had a head loaded with heavy black hair to her shoulders and a white heart-shaped face and wore a skimpy dress with small pink flowers on it. She was so thin that she looked as if she would blow away in fright out of the shop, but instead, pausing on tiptoe she swallowed with appetite: her sharp eyes had seen my red car outside the place. She looked back cautiously at the inner door of the shop and then ran to unlock the door. I went in.

"What are you up to?" I said. "Playing chess?"

"I'm teaching my children," she said, putting up her chin like a child of five. "Do you want to buy something?"

At once Mrs. Price was there, shouting, "Isabel. I told you not to open the door. Go back into the room."

Mrs. Price went to the chessboard and put the pieces back in their places.

"She's a child," said Mrs. Price, accusing me.

And when she said this, Mrs. Price blew herself out to a larger size, then her sullen face went blank and babyish as if she had traveled out of herself for a beautiful moment. Then her brows leveled and she became sullen.

"Mr. August's out," she said.

"It is about a piece of Staffordshire," I said. "He mentioned it to me. When will he be in?"

"He's in and out. No good asking. He doesn't know himself."

"I'll try again."

"If you like."

There was nothing to be got out of Mrs. Price.

In my opinion, the antique trade is not one for a woman, unless she is on her own. Give a woman a shop and she wants to sell something: even the little girl at August's wanted to sell. It's instinct. It's an excitement. Mrs. Price, August's woman, was living with a man exactly like the others in the trade; he hated customers and hated parting with anything. By middle age these women have dead blank faces, they look with resentment and indifference at what is choking their shops; their eyes go smaller and smaller as the chances of getting rid of it become rarer and rarer and they are defeated. Kept out of the deals their husbands have among themselves, they see even their natural love of intrigue frustrated. This was the case of Mrs. Price, who must have been handsome in a big-boned way when she was young, but who had swollen into a drudge. What allured the men did not allure her at all. The trade feeds on illusions. If you go after Georgian silver you catch the illusion, while you are bidding, that you are related to the rich families who owned it. You acquire imaginary ancestors. Or, like Pliny with the piece of Meissen he never got his hands on, you drift into German history and become a secret curator of the Victoria and Albert Museum—a place he often visited. August's lust for "the ivories" gave to his horse-racing mind, a private Oriental side: he dreamed of rajahs, sultans, harems and lavish gamblers, which, in a man as vulgar as he was, came out, in sad reality, as a taste for country girls and the company of bookies. Illusions lead to furtiveness in everyday life and to sudden temptations: the trade is close to larceny, to situations where you don't ask where something has come from, especially for a man like August whose dreams had landed him in low company. He had started at the bottom, and very early he "received" and got twelve months for it. This frightened him. He took up with Mrs. Price and though he resented it she had made a fairly honest man of him. August was to be *her* work of art.

But he did not make an honest woman of her. No one disapproved of this except herself. Her very size, growing year by year, was an assertion of virtue. Everyone took her side in her public quarrels with him. And as if to make herself more respectable, she had taken in her sister's little girl when the sister died: the mother had been in Music Hall. Mrs. Price petted and prinked the little thing. When August became a failure as a work of art, Mrs. Price turned to the child. Even August was charmed by her when she jumped on his knee and danced about showing him her new clothes. A little actress, as everyone said—exquisite.

It took me a long time to give up the belief that August had the Cranmer piece, and as I know now, he hadn't got it; but at last I did see I was wasting my time and settled into the routine of the business. I sometimes saw August at country sales and at one outside Marlborough something ridiculous happened. It was a big sale and went on till late in the afternoon and he had been drinking; after lunch the auctioneer had put up a china cabinet and the bidding was strong. Some outsider was bidding against the dealers, a thing that made them close their faces with moral indignation: the instinctive hatred of customers united them. Drink always stirred August morally; he was a rather despised figure and he was, I suppose, determined to speak for all. He entered the bidding. Up went the price: 50,5,60,5,70,5,80,5,90. The outsiders were a young couple with a dog.

"Ninety, ninety?" called the auctioneer.

August could not stand it. "Twice-five," he shouted.

There is not much full-throated laughter at sales: it is usually shoppish and dusty. But the crowd in this room

looked round at August and shouted with a laughter that
burst the gloom of trade. He was put out for a second
and then saw his excitement had made him famous. The
laughter went on: the wonder had for a whole minute
stopped the sale. "Twice-five!" He was slapped on the
back. At sixty-four the man who had never had a nick-
name had been christened. He looked around him. I saw
a smile cross his face and double the pomposity that beer
had put into him and he redoubled it that evening at the
nearest pub. I went off to my car, and Alsop of Ramsey,
the ephemera man who had picked up some Victorian
programs, followed me and said out of the side of his
mouth, "More trouble tonight at August's."

And then to change the subject and speaking for every
dealer south of the Trent, he offered serious news. "Pliny's mother's dead—Pliny of the Green."

The voice had all the shifty meaning of the trade. I was
too simple to grasp the force of this confidence. It surprised me in the following weeks to hear people repeat
the news, "Pliny's mother's dead," in so many voices,
from the loving-memory-and-deepest-sympathy manner
as much suited to old clothes, old furniture and human
beings indiscriminately as to the flat statement that an
event of business importance had occurred in my event-
less trade. I was in it for the money and so, I suppose,
were all the rest—how else could they live?—but I
seemed to be surrounded by a dreamy free masonry who
thought of it in a different secretive way.

On a wet morning the following spring I was passing
through Salisbury on market day and stopped in the
square to see if there was anything worth picking up at
the stalls there. It was mostly junk, though I did find a
pretty Victorian teapot—no mark, I agree—with a chip in
the spout for a few shillings, because the fever of the
trade never quite leaves one even on dull days. (I sold the
pot five years later for eight pounds when prices started

to go mad). I went into one of the pubs on the square—
I forget its name—and I was surprised to see Marbright
and Alsop there and, sitting near the window, Mrs. Price.
August was getting drinks at the bar.

Alsop said to me, "Pliny's here. I passed him a minute
ago."

Marbright said, "He was standing in Woolworth's
doorway. I asked him to come and have one, but he
wouldn't."

"It's hit him hard, his mother going," Marbright said.
"What's he doing here? Queen Mary's dead."

It was an old joke that Gentleman Pliny had never been
the same since the old Queen had come to his shop some
time back—everyone knew what she was for picking up
things. He only opened on Sundays now and a wealthy
crowd came there in their big cars—a new trend, as Alsop said. August brought the drinks and stood near, for
Mrs. Price spread herself on the bench and never left
much room for anyone else to sit down. He looked restless and glum.

"Where will Pliny be without his mother," Mrs. Price
moaned into her glass and, putting it down, glowered at
August. She had been drinking a good deal.

August ignored her and said, sneering, "He kept her
locked up." There is always a lot of talking about "lock-
ing up" in the trade; people's minds go to their keys.

"It was a kindness," Mrs. August said, "after the burglars got in at Sampson's, three men in a van loading it
up in broad daylight. Any woman of her age would be
frightened."

"It was nothing to do with the burglary," said August,
always sensitive when crime was mentioned. "She was
getting soft in the head. He caught her giving his stuff
away when she was left on her own. She was past it."

Mrs. Price was a woman who didn't like to be con-
tradicted.

"He's a gentleman," said Mrs. Price, accusing August. "He was good to his mother. He took her out every Sunday night of his life. She liked a glass of stout on Sundays."

This was true, though Mrs. Price had not been to London for years and had never seen this event; but all agreed. We live on myths.

"It was her kidneys," moaned Mrs. Price; one outsize woman was mourning another, seeing a fate.

"I suppose that's why he didn't get married, looking after her," said Marbright.

"Pliny! Get married! Don't make me laugh," said August with a defiant recklessness that seemed to surprise even himself. "The last Saturday in every month like a clock striking he was round the pubs in Brixton with old Lal Drake."

And now, as if frightened by what he said, he swanked his way out of the side door of the pub on his way to the gents'.

We lowered our eyes. There are myths, but there are facts. They all knew—even I had heard—that what August said was true, but it was not a thing a sensible man would say in front of Mrs. Price. And—mind you—Pliny standing a few doors down the street. But Mrs. Price stayed calm among the thoughts in her mind.

"That's a lie," she said peacefully, though she was eyeing the door waiting for August to come back.

"I knew his father," said Alsop. We were soon laughing about the ancient Pliny, the Bermondsey boy who began with a barrow shouting "Old iron" in the streets, a man who never drank, never had a bank account— didn't trust banks—who belted his son while his mother "educated him up"—she was a tall woman and the boy grew up like her, tall with a long arching nose and those big red ears that looked as though his parents had pulled him now this way, now that, in their fight over him. She had been a housekeeper in a big house and she had made a son who looked like an old family butler, cockney to the bone, but almost a gentleman. Except, as Alsop said, his way of blowing his nose like a foghorn on the Thames, but sharp as his father. Marbright said you could see the father's life in the store at the back of the shop: it was piled high with what had made the father's money— every kind of old-fashioned stuff.

"Enough to furnish two or three hotels," Alsop said. Mrs. Price nodded.

"Wardrobes, tables . . ." she said.

"A museum," said Marbright. "Helmets, swords. Two fourposters the last time I was there."

"Ironwork. Brass," nodded Mrs. Price mournfully.

"Must date back to the Crimean War," said Marbright.

"And it was all left to Pliny."

There was a general sigh.

"And he doesn't touch it. Rubbish he calls it. He turned his back on it. Only goes in for the best. Hepplewhite, marquetries, his consoles, Regency."

There was a pause.

"And," I said, "his Meissen."

They looked at me as if I were a criminal. They glanced at one another as if asking whether they should call the police. I was either a thief or I had publicly stripped them of all their clothes. I had publicly announced Pliny's lust.

Although Mrs. Price had joined in the conversation, it was in the manner of someone talking in her sleep, for when this silence came she woke up and said in a startled voice, "Lal Drake." And screwing up her fists she got up, and pausing to get ready for a rush, she heaved herself fast to the door by which August had left for the gents' down the alley a quarter of an hour before.

"The other door, missis," someone shouted. But she was through it.

"Drink up," we said and went out by the front door.

I was the last and had a look down the side alley and
there I saw a sight: August with a hand doing up his fly
buttons and the other arm protecting his face. Mrs. Price
was hitting out at him and shouting. The language!

"You dirty sod. I knew it. The girl told me." She was
shouting. She saw me, stopped hitting and rushed at me
in tears and shouted back at him. "The filthy old man."

August saw his chance and got out of the alley and
made for the cars in the square. She let me go, to shout
after him. We were all there, and in Woolworth's doorway was Pliny. Rain was still falling and he looked wet
and all the more alone for being wet. I walked off, and,
I suppose, seeing me go and herself being alone and
giddy in her rage she looked all round and turned her
temper on me. "The girl has got to go," she shouted.

Then she came to her senses.

"Where is August?" August had got to his car and was
driving out of the square. She could do nothing. Then
she saw Pliny. She ran from me to Pliny, from Pliny to
me.

"He's going after the girl," she screamed.

We calmed her down and it was I who drove her home.
(This was when she told me, as the wipers went up and
down on the windshield, that she and August were not
married.) Her tears were like the hissing water we
splashed through on the road. "I'm worried for the child.
I told her, 'Keep your door locked.' I see it's locked every
night. I'm afraid I'll forget and won't hear him if I've had
a couple. She's a kid. She doesn't know anything." I
understood that the face I had always thought was empty
was really filled with the one person she loved: Isabel.

August was not there when we got to their shop. Mrs.
Price went in, and big as she was, she did not knock
anything over.

"Isabel?" she called.

The girl was in the scullery and came out with a wet

plate that dripped on the carpet. In two years she had changed. She was wearing an old dress and an apron, but also a pair of silver high-heeled evening shoes. She had become the slut of the house and her pale skin looked dirty.

"You're dripping that thing everywhere. What have you got those shoes on for? Where did you get them?"

"Uncle Harry, for Christmas," she said. She called August Uncle Harry. She tried to look jaunty as if she had put all her hope in life into those silly evening shoes.

"All right," said Mrs. Price weakly, looking at me to keep quiet and say nothing.

Isabel took off her apron when she saw me. I don't know whether she remembered me. She was still pale, but had the shapeliness of a small young woman. Her eyes looked restlessly and uncertainly at both of us; her chin was firmer but it trembled. She was smiling too, and because I was there and the girl might see an ally in me, Mrs. Price looked with half-kindness at Isabel. But when I got up to go, the girl looked at me as if she would follow me out the door. Mrs. Price got up fast to bar the way. She stood on the doorstep of the shop watching me get into the car, puffing with the inability to say Thank you or Good-bye. If the girl was a child, Mrs. Price was ten times a child, and both of them standing on the doorstep were like children who don't want anyone to go away.

I drove off, and for a few miles I thought about Mrs. Price and the girl, but once settled into the long drive to London, the thought of Pliny supplanted them. I had been caught up in the fever of the trade. Pliny's mother was dead. What was going to happen to Pliny and all that part of the business Pliny had inherited from his father, the stuff he despised and had not troubled himself with very much in his mother's time? I ought to go "over the water"—as we say in London—to have a look at it some-time.

In a few days I went there; I found the idea had occurred to many others. The shop was on one of the main
bus routes in South London, a speckled early Victorian
place with an ugly red-brick store behind it. Pliny's father
had had an eye for a cozy but useful bit of property. Its
windows had square panes (1810) and to my surprise the
place was open and I could see people inside. There was
Pliny with his nose which looked servile rather than distinguished, wearing a long biscuit-colored tweed jacket
with leather pads at the elbows like a cockney sportsman.
There, too, was August with his wet eyes and drinker's
shame, Mrs. Price swelling over him in her best clothes,
and the girl. They had come up from the country and
August had had his boots cleaned. The girl was in her
best, too, and was standing apart touching things in the
shop and on the point of merriment, looking with wonder at Pliny's ears. He often seemed to be talking at her
when he was talking to Mrs. Price. I said, "Hullo! Up
from the country? What are you doing here?"

Mrs. Price was so large that she had to turn her whole
body and place her belly in front of everyone who spoke
to her.

"Seeing to his teeth," she said, nodding at August, and
from years of habit, August turned, too, when his wife
turned, in case it was just as well not to miss one of her
pronouncements, whatever else he might dodge. One
side of August's jaw was swollen. Then Mrs. Price slowly
turned her whole body to face Pliny again. They were
talking about his mother's death. Mrs. Price was greedy,
as one stout woman thinking of another, for a melancholy tour of the late mother's organs. The face of the
girl looked prettily wise and holidayfied because the
heavy curls of her hair hung close to her face. She looked
out of the window, restless and longing to get away while
her elders went on talking, but she was too listless to do
so. Then she would look again at Pliny's large ears with

a child's pleasure in anything strange: they gave him a doglike appearance, and if the Augusts had not been there, I think she would have jumped at him mischievously to touch them but remembered in time that she had lately grown into a young lady. When she saw him looking at her she turned her back and began writing in the dust on a little table standing next to a cabinet which had a small jug in it. She was writing her name in the dust I S A B . . . And then stopped. She turned round suddenly because she saw I had been watching.

"Is that old Meissen?" she called out, pointing to the jug. They stopped talking. It was comic to see her pretending, for my benefit, that she knew all about porcelain.

"Cor! Old Meissen!" said August, pulling his racing newspaper out of his jacket pocket with excitement, and Mrs. Price fondly swung her big handbag; all laughed loudly—a laugh of lust and knowledge. They knew, or thought they knew, that Pliny had a genuine Meissen piece somewhere, probably upstairs where he lived. The girl was pleased to have made them laugh at her; she had been noticed.

Pliny said decently, "No, dear. That's Caughley. Would you like to see it?"

He walked to the cabinet and took the jug down and put it on a table.

"Got the leopard?" said August knowingly. Pliny showed the mark of the leopard on the base of the jug and put it down again. It was a pretty shapely jug with a spray of branches and in the branches a pair of pheasants were perching, done in transfer. The girl scared us all by picking it up in both hands, but it was charming to see her holding it up and studying it.

"Careful," said Mrs. Price.

"She's all right," said Pliny. Then—it alarmed us—she wriggled with laughter.

"What a funny face," she said.

Under the lip of the jug was the small face of an old man with a long nose looking sly and wicked.

"They used to put a face under the lip," Pliny said.

"That's right," said August.

The girl held it out at arm's length, and looking from the jug to Pliny, she said, "It's like you, Mr. Pliny."

"Isabel!" said Mrs. Price. "That's rude."

"But it is," said Isabel. "Isn't it?" She was asking me. Pliny grinned. We were all relieved to see him take the jug from her and put it back in the cabinet.

"It belonged to my mother," he said. "I keep it there."

Pliny said to me, despising me because I had said nothing and because I was a stranger, "Go into the back and have a look round if you want to. The light's on."

I left the shop and went down the steps into the long storeroom, where the whitewashed walls were gray with dust. There was an alligator hanging by a nail near the steps, a couple of cavalry helmets and a dirty drum that must have been there since the Crimean War. I went down into streets of stacked-up furniture. I felt I was walking into an inhuman crypt or, worse still, one of those charnel houses or ossuaries I had seen pictures of in one of my father's books when I was a boy. Large as the store was, it was lit by a single electric light bulb hanging from a girder in the roof, and the yellow light was deathly. The notion of "picking up" anything at Pliny's depressed me, so that I was left with a horror of the trade I had joined. Yet feelings of this kind are never simple. After half an hour I left the shop.

I understood before that day was over and I was back in the room over my own place that what had made me more wretched was the wound of a sharp joy. First, the sight of the girl leaving her name unfinished in the dust had made my heart jump; then when she held the vase in her hands I had felt the thrill of a revelation: until then

I had never settled what I should go in for, but now I saw
it. Why not collect Caughley? That was it. Caughley: it
was one of those inspirations that excite one so that
every sight in the world changes—even houses, buses,
streets and people are transfigured and become unreal
as desire carries one away—and then, cruelly, it passes
and one is left exhausted. The total impossibility of an
impatient young man like myself collecting Caughley,
which hadn't been made since 1821, became brutally
clear. Too late for Staffordshire, too late for Dresden,
too late for Caughley and all the beautiful things. I was
savage for lack of money. The following day I went to the
Victoria and Albert and there I saw other far more
beautiful things enshrined and inaccessible. I gazed with
wonder. My longing for possession held me, and then I
was elevated to a state of worship, as if they were idols,
holy and never to be touched. Then I remembered the
girl's hands and a violent daydream passed through my
head: it lasted only a second or two, but in that time I
smashed the glass case, grabbed a treasure and bolted
with it. It frightened me that such an idea could have
occurred to me. I left the museum and I turned against
my occupation, against Marbright, Alsop and, above all,
Pliny and August, and it broke my heart to think of that
pretty girl living among such people and drifting into the
shabbiness of the trade. I S A B—half a name, written by
a living finger in dust.

One has these brief sensations when one is young.
They pass and one does nothing about them. There is
nothing remarkable about Caughley—except that you
can't get it. I did not collect Caughley for a simple reason: I had to collect my wits. The plain truth is that I was
incompetent. I had only to look at my bank account. I
had bought too much.

At the end of the year it seemed like the bankruptcy
court unless I had a stroke of luck. Talk of trouble mak-

ing the trade move: I was trouble myself; dealers could
smell it coming and came sniffing into my shop—and at
the end of the year I sold up for what I could get. It would
have been better if I could have waited for a year or two
when the boom began. For some reason I kept the teapot
I had bought in Salisbury to remind me of wasted time.
In its humble way it was pretty.

In the next six months I changed. I had to. I pocketed
my pride and got a dull job at an auctioneer's; at least it
took me out of the office when I got out keys and showed
people round. The firm dealt in house property and
developments. The word "develop" took hold of me.
The firm was a large one and sometimes "developed" far
outside London. I was told to go and inspect some of the
least important bits of property that were coming into
the market. One day a row of shops in Steepleton came
up for sale. I said I knew them. They were on the London
road opposite the Lion Hotel at the end of the town. My
boss was always impressed by topography and the names
of hotels and sent me down there. The shops were in the
row where August and one or two others had had their
business, six of them.

What a change! The Lion had been repainted; the
little shops seemed to have got smaller. In my time the
countryside had begun at the end of the row. Now build-
ers' scaffolding was standing in the fields beyond. I
looked for August's. A cheap café had taken over his
place. He had gone. The mirror man who lived next door
was still there but had gone into beads and fancy art
jewelery. His window was full of hanging knickknacks
and mobiles.

"It's the tourist trade now," he said. He looked ill.

"What happened to August?"

He studied me for a moment and said, "Closed
down," and I could get no more out of him. I crossed the
street to the Lion. Little by little, a sentence at a time in

a long slow suspicious evening, I got news of August
from the barmaid as she went back and forth serving
customers, speaking in a low voice, her eye on the new
proprietor in case the next sentence that came out of her
might be bad for custom. The sentences were spoken
like sentences from a judge summing up, bit by bit. August had got two years for receiving stolen goods; the
woman—"She wasn't his wife"—had been knocked
down by a car as she was coming out of the bar at night
—"not that she drank, not really drank; her weight,
really"—and then came the final sentence that brought
back to me the alerting heat and fever of the trade's
secrets: "There was always trouble over there. It started
when the girl ran away."

"Isabel?" I said.

"I dunno—the girl."

I stood outside the hotel and looked to the east and
then to the west. It was one of those quarters of an hour
on a main road when, for some reason, there is no traffic
coming either way. I looked at the now far-off fields
where the February wind was scything over the grass,
turning it into waves of silver as it passed over them. I
thought of Isab . . . running with a case in her hand, three
years ago. Which way? Where do girls run to? Sad.

I went back to London. There are girls in London too,
you know. I grew a beard, reddish; it went with the red
car, which I had managed to keep. I could afford to take
a girl down to the south coast now and then. Sometimes
we came back by the Brixton road, sometimes through
Camberwell, and when we did this I often slowed down
at Pliny's and told the girls, "That man's sitting on a gold
mine." They never believed it or, at least, only one did.
She said: "Does he sell rings? Let us have a look."

"They're closed," I said. "They're always closed."

"I want to look," she said, so we stopped and got out.
We looked into the dark window—it was Saturday

night—and we could see nothing, and as we stared we
heard a loud noise coming, it seemed, from the place
next door or from down the drive-in at the side of Pliny's
shop, a sound like someone beating boxes or bathtubs at
first until I got what it was: drums. Someone blew a
bugle, a terrible squeaky sound. There was heavy traffic
on the street, but the bugle seemed to split it in half.

"Boys' Brigade, practicing for Sunday," I said. We
stood laughing with our hands to our ears as we stared
into the dark. All I could make out was something white
on a table at the back of the shop. Slowly I saw it was a
set of chessmen. Chess, ivories, August—perhaps Pliny
had got August's chessmen.

"What a din!" said the girl. I said no more to her, for
in my mind there was the long-forgotten picture of Isabel's finger on the pieces, at Steepleton.

When I've got time, I thought, I will run over to Pliny's; perhaps he will know what happened to the girl.

And I did go there again, one afternoon, on my own.
Still closed. I rattled the door handle. There was no
answer. I went to a baker's next door, then to a butcher's,
then to a pub. The same story. "He only opens on Sundays" or "He's at a sale." Then to a tobacconist's. I said
it was funny to leave a shop empty like that, full of valuable stuff. The tobacconist became suspicious.

"There's someone there, all right. His wife's there."

"No, she's not," his wife said. "They've gone off to a
sale. I saw them."

She took the hint.

"No one in charge to serve customers," she said.

I said I'd seen a chessboard that interested me and the
tobacconist said: "It's dying out. I used to play."

"I didn't know he got married," I said.

"He's got beautiful things," said his wife. "Come on
Sunday."

Pliny married! That made me grin. The only women

in his life I had ever heard of were his mother and the gossip about Lal Drake. Perhaps he had made an honest woman of *her*. I went back for one last look at the chessmen and, sure enough, as the tobacconist's wife had hinted, someone *had* been left in charge, for I saw a figure pass through the inner door of the shop. The watcher was watched. Almost at once I heard the tap and roll of a kettledrum; I put my ear to the letter box and distinctly heard a boy's voice shouting orders. Children! All the drumming I had heard on Saturday had come from Pliny's—a whole family drumming. Think of Pliny married to a widow with kids: he had not had time to get his own. I took back what I had thought of him and Lal Drake. I went off for an hour to inspect a house that was being sold on Camberwell Green, and stopped once more at Pliny's on the way back, on the chance of catching him and I went to the window. Standing in the middle of the shop was Isabel.

Her shining black hair went to her shoulders. She was wearing a red dress with a schoolgirlish white collar to it. If I had not known her by her heart-shaped face and her full childish lips, I would have known her by her tiptoe way of standing like an actress just about to sing a song or do a dance when she comes forward on the stage. She looked at me daringly. It was the way, I remembered, she had looked at everyone. She did not know me. I went to the door and tipped the handle. It did not open. I saw her watching the handle move. I went on rattling. She straightened and shook her head, pushing back her hair. She did not go away: she was amused by my efforts. I went back to the window of the shop and asked to come in. She could not hear, of course. My mouth was opening and shutting foolishly. That amused her even more. I pointed to something in the window, signaling that I was interested in it. She shook her head again. I tried pointing to other things: a cabinet, an em-

broidered fire screen, a jar three feet high. At each one
she shook her head. It was like a guessing game. I was
smiling, even laughing, to persuade her. I put my hands
to my chest and pretended to beg like a dog. She laughed
at this and looked behind, as if calling to someone. If
Pliny wasn't there, his wife might be, or the children, so
I pointed upward and made a movement of my hands,
imitating someone turning a key in a lock. I was signaling
"Go and get the key from Mrs. Pliny," and I stepped back
and looked up at a window above the shop. When I did
this, Isabel was frightened; she went away shouting to
someone. And that was the end of it; she did not come
back.

I went away thinking, Well, that is a strange thing!
What ideas people put into your head and you build
fancies yourself: that woman in the bar at Steepleton
telling me Isabel had run away and I imagining her running in those poor evening shoes I'd once seen, in the
rain down the Bath road, when—what was more natural
in a trade where they all live with their hands in one
another's pockets—Pliny had married, and they had
taken the girl on at the shop. It was a comfort to think
of. I hadn't realized how much I had worried about what
would happen to a naïve girl like Isabel when the
breakup came. Alone in the world! How silly. I thought,
One of these Sundays I'll go up there and hear the whole
story. And I did.

There was no one there except Pliny and his rich Sunday customers. I even went into the store at the back,
looked everywhere. No sign of Isabel. The only female
was a woman in a shabby black dress and not wearing a
hat who was talking to a man testing the door of a wardrobe, making it squeak, while the woman looked on without interest, in the manner of a dealer's wife: obviously
the new Mrs. Pliny. She turned to make way for another
couple waiting to look at it. I nearly knocked over a stack
of cane chairs as I got past.

If there was no sign of Isabel, the sight of Pliny shocked me. He had been a dead man, permanently dead as wood, even clumsy in his big servile bones, though shrewd. Now he had come to life in the strangest, excited way—much older to look at, thinner and frantic as he looked about him this way and that. He seemed to be possessed by a demon. He talked loudly to people in the shop and was suspicious when he was not talking. He was frightened, abrupt, rude. Pliny married! Marriage had wrecked him or he was making too much money; he looked like a man expecting to be robbed. He recognized me at once. I had felt him watching me from the steps going down to the store. As I came back to the steps to speak to him he spoke to me first—distinctly, in a loud voice, "I don't want any of August's men here, see?"

I went red in the face. "What do you mean?" I said.

"You heard me," he said. "You know what he got."

Wells of Hungerford was standing near, pretending not to listen. Pliny was telling the trade that I was in with August—publicly accusing me of being a fence. I controlled my temper.

"August doesn't interest me," I said. "I'm in property. Marsh, Help and Hitchcock. I sold his place, the whole street."

And I walked past him looking at a few things as I left.

I was in a passion. The dirty swine—all right when his mother kept an eye on him, the poor old woman, but now, he'd gone mad. And that poor girl! I went to the tobacconist's for the Sunday paper in a dream, put down my money and took it without a word and was almost out the door when the wife called out, "Did you find him? Did you get what you wanted?" A friendly London voice. I tapped the side of my head.

"You're telling me," the wife said. "Well, he has to watch everything now. Marrying a young girl like that, it stands to reason," she said in a melancholy voice.

"Wears him out, at his age," suggested the tobacconist.

"Stop the dirty talk, Alfred," said the wife.

"You mean he married the *girl?*" I said. "Who's the big woman without a hat—in the store?"

"What big woman is that?" asked the tobacconist's wife. "He's married to the girl. Who else do you think—there's no one else."

The wife's face went as blank as a tombstone in the sly London way.

"She's done well for herself," said the tobacconist. "Keeps her locked up like his mother, wasn't I right?"

"He worships her," said the woman.

I went home to my flat. I was nauseated. The thought of Isabel in bed with that dressed-up servant, with his wet eyes, his big raw ears and his breath smelling of onions! Innocent? No, as the woman said, "She has done well for herself." Happy with him too. I remembered her pretty face laughing in the shop. What else could you expect, after August and Mrs. Price.

The anger I felt with Pliny grew to a rage, but by the time I was in my own flat, Pliny vanished from the picture in my mind. I was filled with passion for the girl. The fever of the trade had come alive in me: Pliny had got something I wanted. I could think of nothing but her, just as I remember the look August gave Pliny when the girl asked if the jug was Meissen. I could see her holding the jug at arm's length, laughing at the old man's face under the lip. And I could see that Pliny was not mad: what was making him frantic was possessing the girl.

I kept away from Pliny's. I tried to drive the vision out of my mind, but I could not forget it. I became cunning. Whenever my job allowed it—and even when it didn't—I started passing the time of day with any dealer I had known, picked up news of the sales, studied catalogs, tried to find out which ones Pliny would go to. She might

be with him. I actually went to Newbury but he was not
there. Bath he couldn't miss and, sure enough, he was
there and she wasn't. It was ten in the morning and the
sale had just started.

I ran off and got into my car. I drove as fast as I could
the hundred miles back to London and cursed the lunchtime traffic. I got to Pliny's shop and rang the bell. Once,
then several long rings. At once the drum started beating
and went on as if troops were marching. People passing
in the street paused to listen too. I stood back from the
window and I saw a movement at a curtain upstairs. The
drumming was still going on, and when I bent to listen
at the letter box I could hear the sound become deafen-
ing and often very near and then there was a blast from
the bugle. It was a misty day south of the river, and for
some reason or other I was fingering the gray window
and started writing her name, I S A B . . . hopelessly, but
hoping that perhaps she might come near enough to see.
The drumming stopped. I waited and waited and then I
saw an extraordinary sight: Isabel herself in the dull-red
dress, but with a lancer's helmet on her head and a side
drum on its straps hanging from her shoulders and the
drum sticks in her hand. She was standing upright like a
boy playing soldiers, her chin up and puzzling at the
sight of the letters ᗺA2I on the window. When she saw
me she was confused. She immediately gave two or three
taps to the drum and then bent almost double with
laughter. Then she put on a straight face and played the
game of pointing to one thing after another in the shop.
Every time I shook my head, until at last I pointed to her.
This pleased her. Then I shouted through the letter box,
"I want to come in."

"Come in," she said. "It's open." The door had been
open all the time: I had not thought of trying it. I went
inside.

"I thought you were locked in."

She did not answer but wagged her head from side to side.

"Sometimes I lock myself in," she said. "There are bad people about, August's men."

She said this with an air of great importance, but her face became ugly as she said it. She took off the helmet and put down the drum.

"So I beat the drum when Mr. Pliny is away," she said. She called him Mr. Pliny.

"What good does that do?"

"It is so quiet when Mr. Pliny is away. I don't do it when he's here. It frightens August's men away."

"It's as good as telling them you are alone here," I said. "That's why I came. I heard the drum and the bugle."

"Did you?" she said eagerly. "Was it loud?"

"Very loud."

She gave a deep sigh of delight.

"You see!" she said, nodding her head complacently.

"Who taught you to blow the bugle?" I said.

"My mother did," she said. "She did it on the stage. Mr. Pliny—you know, when Mr. Pliny fetched me in his motorcar—I forgot it. He had to go back and get it. I was too frightened."

"Isab . . ." I said.

She blushed. She remembered.

"I might be one of August's men," I said.

"No, you're not. I know who you are," she said. "Mr. Pliny's away for the day but that doesn't matter. I am in charge. Is there something you were looking for?"

The child had gone when she put the drum aside. She became serious and practical: Mrs. Pliny! I was confused by my mistake in not knowing the door was open and she busied herself about the shop. She knew what she was doing and I felt very foolish.

"Is there something special?" she said. "Look

around." She had become a confident woman. I no longer felt there was anything strange about her. I drifted to look at the chessmen and I could not pretend to myself that they interested me, but I did ask her the price. She said she would look it up and went to a desk where Pliny kept his papers, and after going through some lists of figures which were all in code she named the sum. It was enormous—something like £275 and I said "What!" in astonishment. She put the list back on the desk and said firmly, "My husband paid two hundred and sixty pounds for it last Sunday. It was carved by Dubois. There are only two more like it. It was the last thing he did in 1785."

(I found out afterwards this was nonsense.)

She said this in Pliny's voice; it was exactly the sort of casual sentence he would have used. She looked expressionless and not at all surprised when I said, "Valuable," and moved away.

I meant, of course, that she was valuable, and in fact her mystery having gone, she seemed conscious of being valuable and important herself, the queen and owner of everything in the shop, efficiently in charge of her husband's things. The cabinet in the corner, she said, in an offhand way, as I went to look at it, had been sold to an Australian. "We are waiting for the packers." We! Not to feel less knowing than she was, I looked around for some small thing to buy from her. There were several small things, like a cup and saucer, a little china tray, a christening mug. I picked things up and put them down listlessly, and from being indifferent she became eager and watched me. The self-important, serious expression she had had vanished, she became childish suddenly and anxious: she was eager to sell something. I found a little china figure on a shelf.

"How much is this?" I said. It was Dresden: the real thing. She took it and looked at the label. I knew it was far beyond my purse and I asked her the price in the bored hopeless voice one puts on.

"I'll have to look it up," she said.

She went to the desk again and looked very calculating and thoughtful and then said, as if naming an enormous sum, "Two pounds."

"It can't be," I said.

She looked sad as I put it back on the shelf and she went back to the desk. Then she said, "I tell you what I'll do. It's got a defect. You can have it for thirty-five shillings."

I picked it up again. There was no defect in it. I could feel the huge wave of temptation that comes to one in the trade, the sense of the incredible chance, the lust that makes one shudder first and then breaks over one so that one is possessed, though even at that last moment, one plays at delay in a breathless pause now that one is certain of one's desire.

I said, "I'll give you thirty bob for it."

Young Mrs. Pliny raised her head and her brown eyes became brilliant with naïve joy.

"All right," she said.

The sight of her wrapping the figure, packing it in a box and taking the money so entranced me, that I didn't realize what she was doing or what I had done. I wasn't thinking of the figure at all; I was thinking of her. We shook hands. Hers were cold and she waved from the shop door when I left. And when I got to the end of the street and found myself holding the box I wondered why I had bought it. I didn't want it. I had felt the thrill of the thief and I was so ashamed that I once or twice thought of dropping it into a litter box. I even thought of going back and returning it to her and saying to her, "I didn't want it. It was a joke. I wanted you. Why did you marry an awful old man like Pliny?" And those stories of Pliny going off once a month in the old days, in his mother's

time, to Lal Drake, that old whore in Brixton, came back
to me. I didn't even unpack the figure but put it on the
mantelpiece in my room, then on the top shelf of a cupboard which I rarely used. I didn't want to see it. And
when in the next months—or even years—I happened to
see it, I remembered her talking about the bad people,
August's men.

But though I kept away from Pliny's on Sundays, I
could not resist going back to the street and eventually
to the shop—just for the sight of her.

And after several misses I did see her in the shop. It
was locked. When I saw her she stared at me with fear
and made no signals and quickly disappeared—I suppose, into the room at the back. I crossed the main road
and looked at the upper part of the house. She was upstairs, standing at a window. So I went back across the
street and tried to signal, but, of course, she could only
see my mouth moving. I was obsessed by the way I had
cheated her. My visits were a siege, for the door was
never open now. I did see her once through the window
and this time I had taken the box and offered it to her
in dumb show. That did have an effect. I saw she was
looking very pale, her eyes ringed and tired and whether
she saw I was remorseful or not I couldn't tell, but she
made a rebuking yet defiant face. Another day I went and
she looked terrified. She pointed and pointed to the
door, but as I eagerly stepped towards it she shook her
head and raised a hand to forbid me. I did not understand until, soon, I saw Pliny walking about the shop. I
moved off. People in the neighborhood must often have
seen me standing there and the tobacconist I went to
gave me a look that suggested he knew what was going
on.

Then, on one of my vigils, I saw a doctor go to the side
door down the goods entrance and feared she was ill, but
the butcher told me it was Pliny. His wife, they said, had

been nursing him. He ought to convalesce somewhere.
"A nice place by the sea. But he won't. It would do his
wife good. The young girl has worn herself out looking
after him. Shut up all day with him." And the tobacconist
said what his wife had said a long time back. "Like his
poor mother. He kept *her* locked in too. Sunday evening's the only time she's out. It's all wrong."

I got sick of myself. I didn't notice the time I was
wasting, for one day passed like a smear of gray into
another and I wished I could drag myself away from the
district, especially now that Pliny was always there. At
last, one Saturday, I fought hard against a habit so useless and I had the courage to drive past the place for once
and not park my car up the street. I drove on, taking side
streets (which I knew, nevertheless, would lead me back),
but I made a mistake with the one-ways and got on the
main Brixton road and was heading north to freedom
from myself.

It was astonishing to be free. It was seven o'clock in the
evening, and to celebrate I went into a big pub where
they had singers on Saturday nights; it was already filling
up with people. How normal, how cheerful they were, a
crowd of them, drinking, shouting and talking: the human race! I got a drink and chose a quiet place in a
corner and I was taking my first mouthful of the beer,
saying to myself: "Here's to yourself, my boy," as though
I had just met myself as I used to be. And then, with the
glass still at my lips, I saw in a crowd at the other end of
the bar Pliny, with his back half turned. I recognized him
by his jug-handle ears, his white hair, and the stoop of
a tall man. He was not in his dressy clothes but in a
shabby suit that made him seem disguised. He was listening to a woman with a large handbag who had bright
blond hair and a big red mouth; she was telling him a
joke and she banged him in the stomach with her bag and
laughed. Someone near me said, "Lal's on the job early

this evening." Lal Drake. All the old stories about Pliny and his woman came back to me and how old Castle of Westbury said that Pliny's mother had told him, when she was saying what a good son he was to her, that the one and only time he had been with a woman he had come home and told her and put his head in her lap and cried "like a child" and promised on the Bible he'd never do such a thing again. Castle swore this was true.

I put down my glass and got out of the pub fast without finishing it. Not because I was afraid of Pliny. Oh no! I drove straight back to Pliny's shop. I rang the bell. The drum started beating a few taps and then a window upstairs opened.

"What do you want?" said Isabel in a whisper.

"I want to see you. Open the door."

"It's locked."

"Get the key."

She considered me for a long time.

"I haven't got one," she said, still in a low voice, so hard to hear that she had to say it twice.

"Where have you been?" she said.

We stared at each other's white faces in the dark. She had missed me!

"You've got a key. You must have," I said. "Somewhere. What about the back door?"

She leaned on the window, her arms on the sill. She was studying my clothes.

"I have got something for you," I said. This changed her. She leaned forward, trying to see more of me in the dark. She was curious. Today I understand what I did not understand then: she was looking me over minutely, inch by inch—what she could see of me in the sodium light of the street lamp—not because I was strange or unusual but because I was not. She had been shut up either alone or with Pliny without seeing another soul for so long. He was treating her like one of his collector's pieces, like the

Meissen August had said he kept hidden upstairs. She closed the window. I stood there wretched and impatient. I went down the goods entrance ready to kick the side door down, break a window, climb in somehow. The side door had no letter box or glass panes, no handle even. I stood in front of it and suddenly it was opened. She was standing there.

"You're *not* locked in," I said.

She was holding a key.

"I found it," she said.

I saw she was telling a lie.

"Just now?"

"No. I know where he hides it," she said, lowering her frank eyes.

It was a heavy key with an old piece of frayed used-up string on it.

"Mr. Pliny does not like me to show people things," she said. "He has gone to see his sister in Brixton. She is very ill. I can't show you anything."

She recited these words as if she had learned them by heart. It was wonderful to stand so near to her in the dark.

"Can I come in?" I said.

"What do you want?" she said cautiously.

"You," I said.

She raised her chin.

"Are you one of August's men?" she said.

"You know I'm not. I haven't seen August for years."

"Mr. Pliny says you are. He said I was never to speak to you again. August was horrible."

"The last I heard he was in prison."

"Yes," she said. "He steals." This seemed to please her: she forgave him that easily. Then she put her head out of the doorway as if to see if August were waiting behind me.

"He does something else too," she said.

I remembered the violent quarrel between August and

poor Mrs. Price when she was drunk in Salisbury—the
quarrel about Isabel.

"You ran away," I said.

She shook her head.

"I didn't run away. Mr. Pliny fetched me," she said and
nodded primly, "in his car. I told you."

Then she said, "Where is the present you were bringing me?"

"It isn't a present," I said. "It's the little figure I
bought from you. You didn't charge me enough. Let me
in. I want to explain."

I couldn't bring myself to tell her that I had taken
advantage of her ignorance, so I said, "I found out afterwards that it was worth much more than I paid you. I
want to give it back to you."

She gave a small jump towards me. "Oh please,
please," she said and took me by the hand. "Where is
it?"

"Let me come in," I said, "and I will tell you. I haven't
got it with me. I'll bring it tomorrow—no, not tomorrow
—Monday."

"Oh. Please," she pleaded. "Mr. Pliny was so angry
with me for selling it. He'd never been angry with me
before. It was terrible. It was awful."

It had never occurred to me that Pliny would even
know she had sold the piece; but now I remembered the
passions of the trade and the stored-up lust that seems
to pass between things and men like Pliny. He wouldn't
forgive. He would be savage.

"Did he do something to you? He didn't hit you, did
he?"

Isabel did not answer.

"What did he do?"

I remembered how frantic Pliny had been and how
violent he had sounded when he told me to get out of his
shop.

"He cried," she said. "He cried and he cried. He went

down on his knees and he would not stop crying. I was wicked to sell it. I am the most precious thing he has. Please bring it. It will make him better."

"Is he still angry?"

"It has made him ill," she said.

"Let me come in," I said.

"Will you promise?"

"I swear I'll bring it," I said.

"For a minute," she said, "but not in the shop."

I followed her down a dark passage into the store and was so close that I could smell her hair.

Pliny crying! At first I took this to be one of Isabel's fancies. Then I thought of tall, clumsy, servantlike Pliny —expert at sales with his long-nosed face pouring out water like a pump—acting repentant, remorseful, agonized like an animal to a pretty girl. Why? Just because she had sold something? Isabel loved to sell things. He must have had some other reason. I remembered Castle of Westbury's story. What had he done to the girl? Only a cruel man could have gone in for such an orgy of self-love. He had the long face on which tears would be a blackmail. He would be like a horse crying because it had lost a race.

Yet those tears were memorable to Isabel and she so firmly called him "Mr. Pliny." In bed, did she still call him "Mr. Pliny"? I have often thought since that she did: it would have given her a power—perhaps cowed him.

At night the cold whitewashed storeroom was silent under the light of its single bulb and the place was mostly in shadow; only the tops of stacked furniture stood out in the yellow light, some of them like buildings. The foundations of the stacks were tables or chests, desks on which chairs or small cabinets were piled. We walked down alleys between the stacks. It was like walking through a dead, silent city, abandoned by everyone who once lived there. There was the sour smell of upholstery;

in one part there was a sort of plaza where two large dining tables stood with their chairs set around and a pile of dessert plates on them. Isabel was walking confidently. She stopped by a dressing table with a mirror on it next to a group of wardrobes and turning round to face it, she said proudly, "Mr. Pliny gave it all to me. And the shop."

"All of this?"

"When he stopped crying," she said.

And then she turned about and we faced the wardrobes. There were six or seven, one in rosewood and an ugly yellow one, and they were so arranged here that they made a sort of alcove or room. The wardrobe at the corner of the alley was very heavy and leaned so that its doors were open in a manner of such empty hopelessness, showing its empty shelves, that it made me uneasy. Someone might have just taken his clothes from it in a hurry, perhaps that very minute, and gone off. He might be watching us. It was the wardrobe with the squeaking door which I had seen the customer open while the woman whom I had thought to be Mrs. Pliny stood by. Each piece of furniture seemed to watch—even the small things, like an umbrella stand or a tray left on a table. Isabel walked into the alcove, and there was a greenish-gray sofa with a screwed-up paper bag of toffees on it and on the floor beside it I saw, of all things, the lancer's helmet and the side drum and the bugle. The yellow light scarcely lit this corner.

"There's your drum," I said.

"This is my house," she said, gaily now. "Do you like it? When Mr. Pliny is away I come here in case August's men come . . ."

She looked at me doubtfully when she mentioned that name again.

"And you beat the drum to drive them away?" I said.

"Yes," she said stoutly.

I could not make out whether she was playing the

artless child or not, yet she was a woman of twenty-five
at least. I was bewildered.

"You are frightened here on your own, aren't you?"

"No, I am not. It's nice."

Then she said very firmly, "You will come here on
Monday and give me the box back?"

I said, "I will if you'll let me kiss you. I love you,
Isabel."

"Mr. Pliny loves me too," she said.

"Isab . . ." I said. That did move her.

I put my arm round her waist and she let me draw her
to me. It was strange to hold her because I could feel her
ribs, but her body was so limp and feeble that, loving her
as I did, I was shocked and pulled her tightly against me.
She turned her head weakly so that I could only kiss her
cheek and see only one of her eyes, and I could not make
out whether she was enticing me, simply curious about
my embrace or drooping in it without heart.

"You *are* one of August's men," she said, getting away
from me. "He used to try and get into my bed. After that,
I locked my door."

"Isabel," I said. "I am in love with you. I think you love
me. Why did you marry a horrible old man like Pliny?"

"Mr. Pliny is not horrible," she said. "I love him. He
never comes to my room."

"Then he doesn't love you," I said. "Leaving you
locked up here. And you don't love him."

She listened in the manner of someone wanting to
please, waiting for me to stop.

"He is not a real husband, a real lover," I said.

"Yes, he is," she said proudly. "He takes my clothes
off before I go to bed. He likes to look at me. I am the
most precious thing he has."

"That isn't love, Isabel," I said.

"It is," she said with warmth. "You don't love me. You
cheated me. Mr. Pliny said so. And you don't want to

look at me. You don't think I'm precious."

I went to take her in my arms again and held her.

"I love you. I want you. You are beautiful. I didn't cheat you. Pliny is cheating you, not me," I said. "He is not with his sister. He's in bed with a woman in Brixton. I saw them in a pub. Everyone knows it."

"No, he is not. I *know* he is not. He doesn't like it. He promised his mother," she said.

The voice in which she said this was not her playful voice: the girl vanished and a woman had taken her place —not a distressed woman, not a contemptuous or a disappointed one.

"He worships me," she said, and in the squalid store of dead junk she seemed to be illumined by the simple knowledge of her own value and looked at my love as if it were nothing at all.

I looked at the sofa and was so mad that I thought of grabbing her and pulling her down there. What made me hesitate was the crumbled bag of toffees on it. I was as nonplused and, perhaps, as impotent as Pliny must have been. In that moment of hesitation she picked up her bugle and standing in the aisle, she blew it hard, her cheeks going out full and the noise and echoes seemed to make the shadows jump. I have never heard a bugle call that scared me so much. It killed my desire.

"I told you not to come in," she said. "Go away."

And she walked into the aisle between the furniture, swinging her key to the door.

"Come back," I said as I followed her.

I saw her face in the dressing-table mirror we had passed before, then I saw my own face, red and sweating on the upper lip and my mouth helplessly open. And then in the mirror I saw another face following mine— Pliny's. Pliny must have seen me in the pub.

In that oblong frame of mahogany with its line of yellow inlay, Pliny's head looked winged by his ears and he was coming at me, his head down, his mouth with its yellowing teeth open under the mustache and his eyes stained in the bad light. He looked like an animal. The mirror concentrated him, and before I could do more than half turn he had jumped in a clumsy way at me and jammed one of my shoulders against a tallboy.

"What are you doing here?" he shouted.

The shouts echoed over the store.

"I warned you. I'll get the police on you. You leave my wife alone. Get out. You thought you'd get her on her own and swindle her again."

I hated to touch a white-haired man, but, in pain, I shoved him back hard. We were, as I have said, close to the wardrobe and he staggered back so far that he hit the shelves and the door swung toward him, so that he was half out of my sight for a second. I kicked the door hard with my left foot and it swung to and hit him in the face. He jumped out with blood on his nose. But I had had time to topple the pile of little cane chairs into the alleyway between us. Isabel saw this and ran round the block of furniture and reached him, and when I saw her she was standing with the bugle raised like a weapon in her hand to defend the old man from me. He was wiping his face. She looked triumphant.

"Don't you touch Mr. Pliny," she shouted at me. "He's ill."

He *was* ill. He staggered. I pushed my way through the fallen chairs and I picked up one and said, "Pliny, sit down on this." Pliny with the bleeding face glared and she forced him to sit down. He was panting. And then a new voice joined us: the tobacconist came down the alley.

"I heard the bugle," he said. "Anything wrong? Oh Gawd, look at his face. What happened, Pliny? Mrs. Pliny, you all right?" And then he saw me. All the native shadiness of the London streets, all the gossip of the neighborhood, came into his face.

"I said to my wife," he said, "something's wrong at Pliny's."

"I came to offer Mr. Pliny a piece of Dresden," I said, "but he was out at Brixton seeing his sister, his wife said. He came back and thought I'd broken in and hit himself on the wardrobe."

"You oughtn't to leave Mrs. Pliny alone with all this valuable stock, Mr. Pliny. Saturday night too," the tobacconist said.

Tears had started rolling down Pliny's cheeks very suddenly when I mentioned Brixton and he looked at me and the tobacconist in panic.

"I'm not interested in Dresden," he managed to say.

Isabel dabbed his face and sent the tobacconist for a glass of water.

"No, dear, you're not," said Isabel.

And to me she said, "We're not interested."

That was the end. I found myself walking in the street. How unreal people looked in the sodium light.

The Marvellous Girl

THE OFFICIAL cere-
mony was coming to an end. Under the sugary chandeliers of what had once been the ballroom of the mansion
to which the Institute had moved, the faces of the large
audience yellowed and aged as they listened to the last
speeches and made one more effort of chin and shoulder
to live up to the gilt, the brocaded panels of the walls and
the ceiling where cherubs, clouds and naked goddesses
romped. Oh, to be up there among them, thought the
young man sitting at the back, but on the platform the
Director was passing from the eternal values of art to the
"gratifying presence of the Minister," to "Lady Brig-
son's untiring energies," the "labors of Professor Exeter
and his panel" in the Exhibition on the floor below.
When he was named the Professor looked with delight
at the audience and played with a thin gold chain he had
taken from his pocket. The three chandeliers gave a
small united flicker as if covering the yawns of the crowd.
The young man sitting at the back stared at the platform
once more, and then, with his hands on his knees, his
elbows out, his eye turned to the nearest door. He was
getting ready to push past the people sitting next to him
and to be the first out—to get out before his wife, who
was on the platform with the speakers. By ill-luck he had
run into her before the meeting and had been trapped

into sitting for nearly two hours, a spectator of his marriage that had come to an end. His very presence there seemed to him an unsought return to one of those patient suicides he used to commit, day after day, out of drift and habit.

To live alone is to expose oneself to accident. He had been drawing on and off all day in his studio and not until the evening had he realized that he had forgotten to eat. Hunger excited him. He took a bus down to an Italian restaurant. It was one of those places where the proprietor came out from time to time to perform a private ballet. He tossed pancakes almost up to the ceiling and then dropped them into a blaze of brandy in the pan— a diversion that often helped the young man with the girls he now sometimes took there. The proprietor was just at the blazing point when two women came into the restaurant in their winter coats and stood still, looking as if they were on fire. The young man quickly gulped down the last of a few coils of spaghetti and stood up and wiped his mouth. The older and smaller of the two women was his wife and she was wearing a wide hat of black fur that made her look shorter than he remembered her. Free of him, she had become bizarre and smaller. Even her eyes had become smaller and, like mice, saw him at once and gave him an alert and busy smile. With her was the tall, calm girl with dark-blue eyes from their office at the Institute, the one she excitedly called "the marvellous girl," the "only one I have ever been able to get on with."

More than two years had gone by since he and his wife had lived together. The marriage was one of those prickly friendships that never succeeded—to *his* astonishment, at any rate—in turning into love, but are kept going by curiosity. It had become at once something called "our situation": a duet by a pair of annoyed hands. What kept them going was an exasperated interest in each other's love affairs, but even unhappiness loses its tenderness and fascination. They broke. At first they saw each other occasionally, but now rarely—except at the Institute where his drawings were shown. They were connected only by the telephone wire which ran under the London pavements and worried its way under the window ledge of his studio. She would ring up, usually late at night.

"I hope it's all right," she'd say wistfully. "Are you alone?"

But getting nothing out of him on that score, she would become brisk and ask for something out of the debris of their marriage, for if marriages come to an end, paraphernalia hangs on. There were two or three divans, a painted cupboard, some rugs rolled up, boxes of saucepans and frying pans, lamps—useful things, stored in the garage under his studio. But as if to revive an intimacy, she always asked for some damaged object; she had a child's fidelity to what was broken: a lampshade that was scorched, an antique coal bucket with one loose leg, or a rug that had been stained by her dog, Leopold, whose paws were always in trouble. Leopold's limp had come to seem to the young man as the animal's response to their hopeless marriage. The only sound object she had ever wanted—and got into a temper about it—was a screwdriver that had belonged to her father, whom she detested.

Now, in the restaurant, she put up a friendly fight from under the wide-brimmed hat.

"I didn't know you still came here," she said.

"I come now and again."

"You must be going to the opening at the Institute."

"No," he said. "I haven't heard of it."

"But I sent you a card," she said. "You must go. Your drawings are in the Exhibition. It's important."

"Three drawings," said the girl warmly.

"Come with us," his wife said.

"No. I can't. I'm just going to pay my bill."

A lie, of course. She peered at his plate as if hoping to read his fortune, to guess at what he was up to. He turned to the girl and said with feeling, "Are you better now?"

"I haven't been ill," said the girl.

"You said she'd been in hospital," he said to his wife.

"No, I didn't," she said. "She went to Scotland for a wedding."

A quite dramatic look of disappointment on the young man's face made the girl laugh and look curiously at him. He had seen her only two or three times and knew nothing much about her, but she was indeed "marvellous." She was not in hospital, she was beautiful and alive. Astounding. Even, in a bewildering way, disappointing.

The waiter saved him and moved them away.

"Enjoy yourselves," said the young man. "I'm going home."

"Good-bye." The girl turned to wave to him as she followed his wife to the table.

It was that Good-bye that did it for him. It was a radiant Good-bye, half laughing; he had seen her tongue and her even teeth as she laughed. Simply seeing him go had brought life to her face. He went out of the restaurant and in the leathery damp of the street he could see the face following him from lamp to lamp. "Good-bye, good-bye," it was still saying. And that was when he changed his mind. An extraordinary force pulled his scattered mind together: he determined to go to the meeting and to send to her, if he could see her in the crowd, a blinding, laughing, absolute Good-bye forever, as radiant as hers.

Now, as he sat there in the crowded hall there was no sign of her. He had worn his eyes out looking for her. She was not on the platform with his wife and the speakers, of course. The Director, whose voice suggested chocolate, was still thanking away when, suddenly, the young man did see her. For the light of the chandeliers quivered again, dimmed to a red cindery glow and then went out, and as people gasped "Oh," came on strongly again and one or two giggled. In that flash when everyone looked up and around, there was a gap between the ranks of heads and shoulders and he saw her brown hair and her broad pale face with its white-rose look, its good-humored chin and the laugh beginning on it. She turned round and she saw him as he saw her. There are glances that are collisions, scattering the air between like glass. Her expression was headlong in open conniving joy at the sight of things going wrong. She was sitting about ten rows in front of him but he was not quick enough to wave, for now, *plonk,* the lights went out for good. The audience dropped en masse into the blackness, the hall sank gurgling to the bottom of the sea and was swamped. Then, outside, a door banged, a telephone rang, feet shuffled and a slow animal grunting and chattering started everywhere and broke into irreverent squeals of laughter.

Men clicked on their lighters or struck matches, and long anarchic shadows shot over the walls. There was the sudden heat of breath, wool, fur and flesh as if the audience had become one body.

"Keep your seats for a moment," the Director said from the darkness like God.

Now was the time to go. Darkness had wiped out the people on the platform. For the young man they had become too intimate. It had seemed to him that his wife, who sat next to her old lover, Duncan, was offering too lavish a sight of the new life she was proposing to live nowadays. Duncan was white-faced and bitter, and they were at their old game of quarreling publicly under their breath while she was tormenting him openly by making eyes at the Professor, who was responding by making his gold chain spin round faster and faster. The wife of the

Director was studying all this and preparing to defend her husband in case the longing in those female eyes went beyond the Professor and settled on him.

How wrong I was about my wife's character, the young man thought. Who would have thought such wistful virginity could become so rampant. The young man said, "Pull yourself together, Duncan. Tell her you won't stand any more of it. Threaten her with Irmgard . . ."

Darkness had abolished it all.

It was not the darkness of the night outside. This darkness had no flabby wet sky in it. It was dry. It extinguished everything. It stripped the eyes of sight: even the solid human rows were lumped together invisibly. One was suddenly naked in the dark from the boots upward. One could feel the hair on one's body growing and in the chatter one could hear men's voices grunting, women's voices going fast, breath going in and out, muscles changing, hearts beating. Many people stood up. Surrounded by animals like himself he, too, stood up, to hunt with the pack, to get out. Where was the girl? Inaccessible, known, near but invisible. Someone had brought a single candle to the desk at which the Director stood like a specter. He said, "It would seem, ladies and gentlemen, that there has been a failure of the . . . I fear the . . . hope to procure the . . ."

There was a rough animal laugh from the audience, and all standing up now, they began to shuffle slowly for the doors.

"Get out of my way. Please let me pass," the young man shouted in a stentorian voice which no one heard, for he was shouting inside himself. "I have got to get to a girl over there. I haven't seen her for nearly a year. I've got to say Good-bye to her for the last time."

And the crowd stuck out their bottoms and their elbows, broadened their backs and grew taller all around him, saying, "Don't push."

A man, addressing the darkness in an educated voice, said, "It is remarkable how calm an English crowd is. One saw it in the Blitz."

The young man knocked over a chair in the next row and in the next, shoving his way into any gap he could find in the clotted mass of fur and wool, and muttering, "I've only spoken to her three times in my life. She is wearing blue and has a broad nose. She lives somewhere in London—I don't know where—all I know is that I thought she was ill but it turns out that she went to a wedding in Scotland. I heard she is going to marry a young man in Canada. Think of a girl like that with a face as composed as a white rose—but a rose that can laugh —taking her low voice to Canada and lying at night among thousands of fir trees and a continent of flies and snow. I have got to get to the door and catch her there and say Good-bye."

He broke through four rows of chairs, trod on feet and pushed, but the crowd was slow and stacked up solid. Hundreds of feet scraped. Useless to say to them, "A fox is among you. I knew when I first saw this girl that she was to be dreaded. I said just now in a poetic way that her skin is the color of a white rose, but it isn't. Her hair has the gloss of a young creature's, her forehead is wide and her eyebrows are soft and arching, her eyes are dark blue and her lips warm and helpless. The skin is really like bread. A marvellous girl—everyone says so—but the sure sign of it is that when I first saw her I was terrified of her. She was standing by an office window watching people in the street below and talking on the telephone and laughing and the laughter seemed to swim all over her dress and her breasts seemed to join in and her waist too, even her long young legs that were continuing the dance she had been at—she was saying—the night before. It was when she turned and saw me that my sadness began.

"My wife was there—it was her office—and she said to me in a whisper, 'She is marvellous, isn't she? The child enjoys herself and she's right. But what fools girls are. Sleep with all the boys you like, don't get married yet, it's a trap, I keep telling her.'

"I decided never to go to that office again."

The crowd shuffled on in the dark. He was choking in the smell of fur coats, clamoring to get past, to get to the door, angrily begging someone to light one more match —"What? Has the world run out of matches and lighters?"—so that he could see her, but they had stopped lighting matches now. He wanted to get his teeth into the coat of a large broad woman in front of him. He trod on her heels.

"I'm sorry," he wanted to say. "I'm just trying to say Good-bye to someone. I couldn't do it before—think of my situation. I didn't care—it didn't matter to me—but there was trouble at the office. My wife had broken with that wretched man Duncan who had gone off with a girl called Irmgard, and when my wife heard of it she made him throw Irmgard over and took him back, and once she'd got him she took up with the Professor—you saw him twiddling his gold chain. In my opinion it's a surprise that the Exhibition ever got going, what with the Professor and Duncan playing Cox and Box in the office. But I had to deliver my drawings. And so I saw this girl a second time. I also took a rug with me, a rug my wife had asked for from the debris. Oh yes, I've got debris.

"The girl got up quickly from her desk when she saw me. I say *quickly*. She was alone and my sadness went. She pointed to the glass door at the end of the room. 'There's a committee meeting. She's in there with her husband and the others.'

"I said—and this will make you laugh, Mrs. Whatever-your-name-is, but please move on—I said, 'But *I* am her husband,' I said.

"With what went on in that office how could the girl have known? I laughed when I said this, laughing at myself. The girl did not blush; she studied me and then she laughed too. Then she took three steps toward me, almost as if she was running—I counted those steps—for she came near enough to touch me on the sleeve of my raincoat. Soft as her face was, she had a broad strong nose. In those three steps she became a woman in my eyes, not a vision, not a sight to fear, a friendly creature, well shaped.

" 'I ought to have known by your voice—when you telephone,' she said. Her mistake made her face shine.

" 'Is the parcel for the Exhibition?' she said.

"I had put it on a chair.

" 'No, it's a rug. It weighs a ton. It's Leopold's rug.

" 'I've got to go,' I said. 'Just say, "It's Leopold's." Leopold is a dog.'

" 'Oh,' she said. 'I thought you meant a friend.'

" 'No. Leopold wants it, apparently. I've got a lot of rugs. I keep them in the garage at my studio. You don't want a rug, do you? As fast as I get rid of them some girl comes along and says, "How bare you floor is. It needs a rug," and brings me one. I bet when I get back I'll find a new one. Or, I could let you have a box of saucepans, a Hoover, a handsaw, a chest of drawers, fire tongs, a towel rail . . .'

"I said this to see her laugh, to see her teeth and her tongue again and to see her body move under its blue dress which was light blue on that day. And to show her what a distance lay between her life and mine.

" 'I've got to go,' I said again, but at the door I said, 'Beds too. When you get married. All in the garage.'

"She followed me to the door and I waved back to her."

To the back of the fur-coated woman he said, "I can be fascinating. It's a way of wiping oneself out. I wish

you'd wipe yourself out and let me pass. I shall never see
her again."

And until this night he had not seen her again. He
started on a large design which he called The Cor-
nucopia. It was, first of all, a small comic sketch of a dust
bin which contained chunks of the rubbish in his garage
—very clever and silly. He scrapped it, and now he made
a large design and the vessel was rather like the girl's
head, but when he came to drawing the fruits of the earth
they were fruits of geometry—hexagons, octagons,
cubes, with something like a hedgehog on top, so he
made the vessel less like a girl's head; the thing drove
him mad the more he worked on it.

September passed into October in the parks and once
or twice cats on the glass roof of the studio lost their
balance and came sliding down in a screech of claws in
the hurly-burly of love.

One night his wife telephoned him.

"Oh God. Trouble," he said when he heard her plaintive voice. He had kept out of her way for months.

"Is it all right? Are you alone?" she said. "Something
awful has happened. Duncan's going to get married
again. Irmgard has got her claws into him. I rang Alex
—he always said I could ring—but he won't come. Why
am I rejected? And you remember that girl—she's gone.
The work piles up."

"To Canada?" he said.

"What on earth makes you say that?" she said in her
fighting voice.

"You said she was."

"You're always putting words into my mouth. She's in
hospital."

"Ill," he said. "How awful. Where is she?"

"How do I know?" she said. "Leopold!"—and now
she was giggling. "Leopold's making a mess again. I
must ring off."

"I'm sorry," he said.

Ill! In hospital! The picture of the girl running toward him in the office came back to him and his eyes were smeared with tears. He felt on his arms and legs a lick of ice and a lick of fire. His body filled with a fever that passed and then came back so violently that he lost his breath. His knees had gone as weak as string. He was in love with the girl. The love seemed to come up from events thousands of years old. The girl herself, he thought, was not young but ancient. Perhaps Egyptian. The skin of her face was not roselike, nor like bread, but like stone roughened by centuries. "I am feeling love," he said, "for the whole of a woman for the first time. No other woman exists. I feel love not only for her face, her body, her voice, her hands and feet but for the street she lives in, the place she was born, her dresses and stockings, her bus journeys, her handbags, her parties, her dances. I don't know where she is. How can I find out? Why didn't I realize this before?"

Squeezed like a rag between the crowd he got to the doorway, and there the crowd bulged and carried him through it backward because he was turning to look for her. Outside the door was an ambitious landing. The crowd was cautiously taking the first steps down the long sweep of this staircase. There was a glimmer of light here from the marble of the walls, and that educated man gripped his arm and said "Mind the steps down" and barred the young man's way. He fought free of the grip and stood against the wall. "Don't be a damn fool," said the educated man, waving his arms about. "If anyone slips down there, the rest of you will pile on top of him." The man now sounded mad. "I saw it in the war. A few at a time. A few at a time," he screamed. And the young man felt the man's spit on his face. The crowd passed him like mourners, undecipherable, but a huge woman turned on him and held him by the sleeves with both hands. "Thornee! Thornee! Where are you? You're leaving me," she whimpered. "Dear girl," said a man behind her. "I am here." She let go, swung round and collided with her husband and grabbed him. "You had your arm round that woman," she said. They faded past. The young man looked for a face. Up the stairs, pushing against the procession going down, a man came up sidling against the wall. Every two or three steps he shouted "Mr. Zagacheck?" Zagacheck, Zagacheck, Zagacheck came nearer and suddenly a mouth bawled into the young man's face with a blast of heavily spiced breath.

"Mr. Zagacheck?"

"I am not Mr. Zagacheck," said the young man in a cold, clear voice, and as he said it the man was knocked sideways.

A woman took the young man's hand and said, "Francis!" and she laughed. She had *named* him. It was the girl, of course. "Isn't this wild? Isn't it marvellous? I saw you. I've been looking for you," she said.

"I have been looking for *you.*"

He interlaced his fingers with her warm fingers and held her arm against his body.

"Are you with your wife?" she said.

"No," he said.

She squeezed his hand, she lifted it and held it under her arm.

"Are you alone?" he said.

"Yes."

"Good," he said. "I thought you'd gone." Under her arm he could feel her breast. "I mean for good, left the country. I came to say Good-bye."

"Oh yes!" she said with enthusiasm and rubbed herself against him. "Why didn't you come to the office?"

He let go of her hand and put his arm round her waist.

"I'll tell you later. We'll go somewhere."

"Yes!" she said again.

"There's another way out. We'll wait here and then slip out by the back way."

The crowd pressed against them. And then he heard his wife's voice, only a foot away from him. She was saying, "I'm not making a scene. It's you. I wonder what has happened to the girl."

"I don't know and I don't care," the man said. "Stop trying to change the subject. Yes or no? Are you?"

The young man stiffened: "This is the test. If the girl speaks the miracle crashes."

She took his arm from her waist and gripped his hand fiercely. They clenched, sticking their nails into each other, as if trying to wound. He heard one of the large buttons on his wife's coat click against a button of his coat. She was there for a few seconds: it seemed to him as long as their marriage. He had not been as close to his wife for years. Then the crowd moved on, the buttons clicked again and he heard her say, "There's only Leopold there."

In a puff of smoke from her cigarette she vanished. The hands of the girl and Francis softened, and he pressed hard against her.

"Now," he whispered. "I know the way."

They sidled round the long wall of the landing, passing a glimmering bust—"Mr. Zagacheck," he said—and came to the corner of a corridor, long and empty, faintly lit by a tall window at the end. They almost ran down it, hand in hand. Twice he stopped to try the door of a room. A third door opened.

"In here," he said.

He pulled her into a large dark room where the curtains had not been drawn, a room that smelled of new carpet, new paint and new furniture. There was the gleam of a desk. They groped to the window. Below was a square with its winter trees and the headlights of cars playing upon them and the crowd scattering across the roads. He put his arms round her and kissed her on the mouth and she kissed him. Her hands were as wild as his.

"You're mad," she said, "this is the Director's room," as he pushed her onto the sofa, but when his hands were on the skin of her leg she said, "Let's go."

"When did you start to love me?" he said.

"I don't know. Just now. When you didn't come. I don't know. Don't ask me. Just now, when you said you loved me."

"But before?"

"I don't know," she said.

And then the lights in the building came on and the lights on the desk and they got up, scared, hot-faced, hot-eyed, hating the light.

"Come on. We must get out," he said.

And they hurried from the lighted room to get into the darkness of the city.

The Lady from Guatemala

Friday afternoon about four o'clock, the week's work done, time to kill: the editor disliked this characterless hour when everyone except his secretary had left the building. Into his briefcase he had slipped some notes for a short talk he was going to give in a cheap London hall, worn by two generations of protest against this injustice or that, before he left by the night plane for Copenhagen. There his real lecture tour would begin and turn into a short holiday. Like a bored cardplayer, he sat shuffling his papers and resented that there was no one except his rude, hardworking secretary to give him a game.

The only company he had in his room—and it was a moody friend—was his portrait hanging behind him on the wall. He liked cunningly to draw people to say something reassuring about the picture. It was "terribly good," as the saying is; he wanted to hear them say it lived up to him. There was a strange air of rivalry in it. It rather overdid the handsome mixture of sunburned satyrlike pagan and shady jealous Christian saint under the happy storm of white hair. His hair had been gray at thirty: at forty-seven, by a stroke of luck, it was silken white. His face was an actor's, the nose carved for dramatic occasions, the lips for the public platform. It was a face both elated and ravaged by the highest beliefs and doubts. He was energized by meeting this image in the morning and, enviously, he said good-bye to it at night. Its nights would be less tormented than his own. Now he was leaving it to run the paper in his absence.

"Here are your tickets." His secretary breezed into the room. "Copenhagen, Stockholm, Oslo, Berlin, Hamburg, Munich—the lot," she said. She was mannerless to the point of being a curiosity.

She stepped away and wobbled her tongue in her cheek. She understood his restless state. She adored him: he drove her mad and she longed for him to go.

"Would you like to know what I've got outside?" she said. She had a malicious streak. "A lady. A lady from Guatemala. Miss Mendoza. She has got a present for you. She worships you. I said you were busy. Shall I tell her to buzz off?"

The editor was proud of his tolerance in employing a girl so sportive and so familiar; her fair hair was thin and looked harassed, her spotty face set off the knowledge of his own handsomeness in face and behavior.

"Guatemala! Of course I must see her!" he exclaimed. "What *are* you thinking about? We ran three articles on Guatemala. Show her in."

"It's your funeral," said the girl and gave a vulgar click with her tongue. The editor was, in her words, "a sucker for foreigners"; she was reminding him that the world was packed with native girls like herself as well.

All kinds of men and women came to see Julian Drood: politicians who spoke to him as if he were a meeting, quarreling writers, people with causes, cranks and accusers. even criminals and the mad. They were opinions to him and he did not often notice what they were like. He knew they studied him and that they would go away boasting: "I saw Julian Drood today and he said . . ." Still, he had never seen any person quite like the one who now walked in. At first, because of her tweed hat, he thought she was a man and would have said she had a mustache. She was a stump, as square as a box, with tarry chopped-off hair, heavy eyebrows and yellow eyes set in her sallow skin like cut glass. She looked like some un-sexed and obdurate statement about the future—or was it the beginning?—of the human race, long in the body, short in the legs and made of wood. She was wearing on this hot day a thick bottle-green velvet dress. Indian blood obviously: he had seen such women in Mexico. She put out a wide hand to him; it could have held a shovel—in fact she was carrying a crumpled brown-paper bag.

"Please sit down," he said. A pair of heavy feet moved her with a surprisingly light skip to a chair. She sat down stiffly and stared without expression, like geography.

"I know you are a very busy man," she said. "Thank you for sparing a minute for an unknown person." She looked formidably unknown.

The words were nothing—but the voice! He had ex-pected Spanish or broken English of some grating kind, but instead he heard the small, whispering, birdlike monotone of a shy English child.

"Yes, I *am* very busy," he said. "I've got to give a talk in an hour and then I'm off to lecture in Copenhagen . . . What can I do for you?"

"Copenhagen," she said, noting it.

"Yes, yes, yes," said the editor. "I'm lecturing on apartheid."

There are people who listen; there are people for whom anything said seems not to be heard but, rather, to be stamped on or printed. She was also receiving the impress of the walls, the books, the desk, the carpet, the windows of the room, memorizing every object. At last, like a breathless child, she said, "In Guatemala I have dreamed of this for years. I'm saying to myself, 'Even if I could just see the *building* where it all happens!' I didn't dare think I would be able to *speak* to Julian Drood. It is like a dream to me. 'If I see him I will tell him,' I said, 'what this building and what his articles have done for my country.' "

"It's a bad building. Too small," he said. "We're thinking of selling it."

"Oh no," she said. "I have flown across the ocean to see it. And to thank you."

The word "thank" came out like a kiss.

"From Guatemala? To thank me?" The editor smiled.

"To thank you from the bottom of our hearts for those articles." The little voice seemed to sing.

"So people read the paper in Guatemala," said the editor, congratulating that country and moving a manuscript to another pile on his desk.

"Only a few," she said. "The important few. You are keeping us alive in all these dark years. You are holding the torch of freedom burning. You are a beacon of civilization in our darkness."

The editor sat taller in his chair. Certainly he was vain, but he was a good man. Virtue is not often rewarded. A nationalist? Or not? he wondered. He looked at the ceiling, where, as usual—for he knew everything—he found the main items of the Guatemalan situation. He ran over them like a tune on the piano. "Financial colonialism," he said, "foreign monopoly, uprooted peasants, rise of nationalism, the dilemma of the mountain people, the problem of the coast. Bananas.

"It is years since I've eaten a banana," he said.

The woman's yellow eyes were not looking at him directly yet. She was still memorizing the room, and her gaze now moved to his portrait. He was dabbling in the figures of the single-crop problem when she interrupted him.

"The women of Guatemala," she said, addressing the portrait, "will never be able to repay their debt to you."

"The women?"

He could not remember: was there anything about women in those articles?

"It gives us hope. 'Now,' I am saying, 'the world will listen,' " she said. "We are slaves. Man-made laws, the priests, bad traditions hold us down. *We* are the victims of apartheid, too."

And now she looked directly at him.

"Ah," said the editor, for interruptions bored him. "Tell me about that."

"I know from experience," said the woman. "My father was Mexican, my mother was an English governess. I know what she suffered."

"And what do you *do?*" said the editor. "I gather you are not married?"

At this sentence, the editor saw that something like a coat of varnish glistened on the woman's wooden face.

"Not after what I saw of my mother's life. There were ten of us. When my father had to go away on business, he locked her and all of us in the house. She used to shout for help from the window, but no one did anything. People just came down the street and stood outside and stared and then walked away. She brought us up. She was worn out. When I was fifteen, he came home drunk and beat her terribly. She was used to that, but this time she died."

"What a terrible story. Why didn't she go to the consul? Why—"

"He beat her because she had dyed her hair. She had fair hair and she thought if she dyed her hair black like the other women he went with, he would love her again," said the childish voice.

"Because she dyed her hair?" said the editor.

The editor never really listened to astonishing stories of private life. They seemed frivolous to him. What happened publicly in the modern world was far more ex-

travagant. So he only half listened to this tale. Quickly,
whatever he heard turned into paragraphs about something else and moved on to general questions. He was
wondering if Miss Mendoza had the vote and which party
she voted for. Was there an Indian bloc? He looked at his
watch. He knew how to appear to listen, to charm, ask a
jolly question and then lead his visitors to the door
before they knew the interview was over.

"It was a murder," said the woman complacently.

The editor suddenly woke up to what she was saying.

"But you are telling me she was *murdered!*" he exclaimed.

She nodded. The fact seemed of no further interest to
her. She was pleased she had made an impression. She
picked up her paper bag and out of it she pulled a tin of
biscuits and put it on his desk.

"I have brought you a present," she said, "with the
gratitude of the women of Guatemala. It is Scottish
shortbread. From Guatemala." She smiled proudly at
the oddity of this fact. "Open it."

"Shall I open it? Yes, I will. Let me offer you one," he
humored her.

"No," she said. "They are for you."

Murder. Biscuits, he thought. She *is* mad.

The editor opened the tin and took out a biscuit and
began to nibble. She watched his teeth as he bit; once
more, she was memorizing what she saw. She was keeping watch. Just as he was going to get up and make a last
speech to her, she put out a short arm and pointed to his
portrait.

"That is not you," she pronounced. Having made him
eat, she was in command of him.

"But it is," he said. "I think it is very good. Don't
you?"

"It is wrong," she said.

"Oh." He was offended and that brought out his
saintly look.

"There is something missing," she said. "Now I am seeing you I know what it is."

She got up.

"Don't go," said the editor. "Tell me what you miss. It was in the Academy, you know."

He was beginning to think she was a fortuneteller.

"I am a poet," she said. "I see vision in you. I see a leader. That picture is the picture of two people, not one. But you are one man. You are a god to us. You understand that apartheid exists for women too."

She held out her prophetic hand. The editor switched to his wise, pagan look and his sunny hand held hers.

"May I come to your lecture this evening?" she said. "I asked your secretary about it."

"Of course, of course, of course. Yes, yes, yes," he said, and walked with her to the outer door of the office. There they said good-bye. He watched her march away slowly, on her thick legs, like troops.

The editor went into his secretary's room. The girl was putting the cover on her typewriter.

"Do you know," he said, "that woman's father killed her mother because she dyed her hair?"

"She told me. You copped something there, didn't you? What d'you bet me she doesn't turn up in Copenhagen tomorrow, two rows from the front?" the rude girl said.

She was wrong. Miss Mendoza was in the fifth row at Copenhagen. He had not noticed her at the London talk and he certainly had not seen her on the plane; but there she was, looking squat, simple and tarry among the tall fair Danes. The editor had been puzzled to know who she was, for he had a poor visual memory. For him, people's faces merged into the general plain lineaments of the convinced. But he did become aware of her when he got down from the platform and when she stood, well planted, on the edge of the small circle where his white head was bobbing to people who were asking him questions. She listened, turning her head possessively and critically to each questioner and then to him, expectantly. She nodded with reproof at the questioner when he replied. She owned him. Closer and closer she came, into the inner circle. He was aware of a smell like nutmeg. She was beside him. She had a long envelope in her hand. The chairman was saying to him, "I think we should take you to the party now." Then people went off in three cars. There she was at the party.

"We have arranged for your friend . . ." said the host, "we have arranged for you to sit next to your friend."

"Which friend?" the editor began. Then he saw her, sitting beside him. The Dane lit a candle before them. Her skin took on, to the editor's surprised eye, the gleam of an idol. He was bored: he liked new women to be beautiful when he was abroad.

"Haven't we met somewhere?" he said. "Oh yes. I remember. You came to see me. Are you on holiday here?"

"No," she said. "I drink at the fount."

He imagined she was taking the waters.

"Fount?" said the editor, turning to others at the table. "Are there many spas here?" He was no good at metaphors.

He forgot her and was talking to the company. She said no more during the evening until she left with the other guests, but he could hear her deep breath beside him.

"I have a present for you," she said before she went, giving him the envelope.

"More biscuits?" he said waggishly.

"It is the opening canto of my poem," she said.

"I'm afraid," said the editor, "we rarely publish poetry."

"It is not for publication. It is dedicated to you."

And she went off.

"Extraordinary," said the editor, watching her go, and, appealing to his hosts, "That woman gave me a poem."

He was put out by their polite, knowing laughter. It often puzzled him when people laughed.

The poem went into his pocket and he forgot it until he got to Stockholm. She was standing at the door of the lecture hall there as he left. He said, "We seem to be following each other around." And to a minister who was wearing a white tie: "Do you know Miss Mendoza from Guatemala? She is a poet," and escaped while they were bowing.

Two days later, she was at his lecture in Oslo. She had moved to the front row. He saw her after he had been speaking for a quarter of an hour. He was so irritated that he stumbled over his words. A rogue phrase had jumped into his mind—"murdered his wife"—and his voice, always high, went up one more semitone and he very nearly told the story. Some ladies in the audience were propping their cheeks on their forefingers as they leaned their heads to regard his profile. He made a scornful gesture at his audience. He had remembered what was wrong. It had nothing to do with murder: he had simply forgotten to read her poem.

Poets, the editor knew, were remorseless. The one sure way of getting rid of them was to read their poems at once. They stared at you with pity and contempt as you read, and argued with offense when you told them which lines you admired. He decided to face her. After the lecture he went up to her.

"How lucky," he said. "I thought you said you were going to Hamburg. Where are you staying? Your poem is on my conscience."

"Yes?" the small girl's voice said. "When will you come and see me?"

"I'll ring you up," he said, drawing back.

"I'm going to hear you in Berlin," she said with meaning.

The editor considered her. There was a look of magnetized inhuman committal in her eyes. They were not so much looking at him as reading him. She knew his future.

Back in the hotel, he read the poem. The message was plain. It began:

> I have seen the liberator
> The foe of servitude
> The godhead.

He read on, skipping two pages, and put out his hand for the telephone. First he heard a childish intake of breath, and then the small determined voice. He smiled at the instrument; he told her in a forgiving voice how good the poem was. The breathing became heavy, like the sound of the ocean. She was steaming or flying to him across the Caribbean, across the Atlantic.

"You have understood my theme," she said. "Women are being history. I am the history of my country."

She went on and boredom settled on him. His cultivated face turned to stone.

"Yes, yes, I see. Isn't there an old Indian belief that a white god will come from the East to liberate the people? Extraordinary, quite extraordinary. When you get back to Guatemala you must go on with your poem."

"I am doing it now. In my room," she said. "You are my inspiration. I am working every night since I saw you."

"Shall I post this copy to your hotel in Berlin?" he said.

"No, give it to me when we meet there."

"Berlin!" the editor exclaimed. Without thinking,

without realizing what he was saying, the editor said, "But I'm *not* going to Berlin. I'm going back to London at once."

"When?" said the woman's voice. "Could I come and talk to you now?"

"I'm afraid not. I'm leaving in half an hour," said the editor. Only when he put the telephone receiver back did the editor realize that he was sweating and that he had told a lie. He had lost his head. Worse, in Berlin, if she was there, he would have to invent another lie.

It *was* worse than that. When he got to Berlin she was not there. It was perverse of him—but he was alarmed. He was ashamed. The shadiness of the saint replaced the pagan on his handsome face; indeed, on the race question after his lecture a man in the audience said he was evasive.

But in Hamburg at the end of the week, her voice spoke up from the back of the hall: "I would like to ask the great man who is filling all our hearts this evening whether he is thinking that the worst racists are the oppressors and deceivers of women."

She delivered her blow and sat down, disappearing behind the shoulders of bulky German men.

The editor's clever smiles went; he jerked back his heroic head as if he had been shot: he balanced himself by touching the table with the tips of his fingers. He lowered his head and drank a glass of water, splashing it on his tie. He looked for help.

"My friends," he wanted to say, "that woman is following me. She has followed me all over Scandinavia and Germany. I had to tell a lie to escape from her in Berlin. She is pursuing me. She is writing a poem. She is trying to force me to read it. She murdered her father—I mean, her father murdered her mother. She is mad. Someone must get me out of this."

But he pulled himself together and sank to that point

of desperation to which the mere amateurs and hams of
public speaking sink.

"A good question," he said. Two irreverent laughs
came from the audience, probably from the American or
English colony. He had made a fool of himself again.
Floundering, he at last fell back on one of those drifting
historical generalizations that so often rescued him. He
heard his voice sailing into the eighteenth century,
throwing in Rousseau, gliding on to Tom Paine and *The
Rights of Man.*

"Is there a way out at the back of this hall?" he said to
the chairman afterward. "Could someone keep an eye on
that woman? She is following me."

They got him out by a back door.

At his hotel a poem was slipped under his door.

> Suckled on Rousseau
> Strong in the divine message of
>   Nature
> Clasp Guatemala in your arms.

"Room 363" was written at the end. She was staying
in the same hotel! He rang down to the desk, said he
would receive no calls and demanded to be put on the
lowest floor, close to the main stairs and near the exit.
Safe in his new room he changed the time of his flight
to Munich.

There was a note for him at the desk.

"Miss Mendoza left this for you," said the clerk, "when
she left for Munich this morning."

Attached to the note was a poem. It began:

> Ravenous in the long night of the centuries
> I waited for my liberator
> He shall not escape me.

His hand was shaking as he tore up the note and the poem and made for the door. The page boy came running after him with the receipt for his bill which he had left on the desk.

The editor was a well-known man. Reporters visited him. He was often recognized in hotels. People spoke his name aloud when they saw it on passenger lists. Cartoonists were apt to lengthen his neck when they drew him, for they had caught his habit of stretching it at parties or meetings, hoping to see and be seen.

But not on the flight to Munich. He kept his hat on and lowered his chin. He longed for anonymity. He had a sensation he had not had for years, not, indeed, since the pre-thaw days in Russia: that he was being followed not simply by one person but by dozens. Who were all those passengers on the plane? Had those two men in raincoats been at his hotel?

He made for the first cab he saw at the airport. At the hotel he went to the desk.

"Mr. and Mrs. Julian Drood," the clerk said. "Yes. Four fifteen. Your wife has arrived."

"My wife!" In any small group the actor in him woke up. He turned from the clerk to a stranger standing at the desk beside him and gave a yelp of hilarity. "But I am not married!" The stranger drew away. The editor turned to a couple also standing there. "I'm saying I am not married," he said. He turned about to see if he could gather more listeners.

"This is ludicrous," he said. No one was interested, and loudly to the clerk he said, "Let me see the register. There is no Mrs. Drood."

The clerk put on a worldly look to soothe any concern about the respectability of the hotel in the people who were waiting. But there, on the card, in her writing, were the words: Mr. and Mrs. J. Drood—London.

The editor turned dramatically to the group.

"A forgery," he cried. He laughed, inviting all to join the comedy. "A woman traveling under my name."

The clerk and the strangers turned away. In travel, one can rely on there being one mad Englishman everywhere.

The editor's face darkened when he saw he had exhausted human interest.

"Four fifteen. Baggage," called the clerk.

A young porter came up quick as a lizard and picked up the editor's bags.

"Wait. Wait," said the editor. Before a young man so smoothly uniformed he had the sudden sensation of standing there with most of his clothes off. When you arrived at the Day of Judgment there would be some worldly youth, humming a tune you didn't know the name of, carrying not only your sins but your virtues indifferently in a couple of bags and gleaming with concealed knowledge.

"I have to telephone," the editor said.

"Over there," said the young man as he put the bags down. The editor did not walk to the telephone but to the main door of the hotel. He considered the freedom of the street. The sensible thing to do was to leave the hotel at once, but he knew that the woman would be at his lecture that night. He would have to settle the matter once and for all now. So he turned back to the telephone booth. It stood there empty, like a trap. He walked past it. He hated the glazed, whorish, hypocritically impersonal look of telephone booths. They were always unpleasantly warmed by the random emotions left behind in them. He turned back: the thing was still empty. "Surely," he wanted to address the people coming and going in the foyer, "someone among you wants to telephone?" It was wounding that not one person there was interested in his case. It was as if he had written an article that no one had read. Even the porter had gone. His two bags rested against the desk. He and they had ceased to be news.

He began to walk up and down quickly, but this stirred no one. He stopped in every observable position, not quite ignored now, because his handsome hair always made people turn.

The editor silently addressed them again. "You've entirely missed the point of my position. Everyone who has read what I have written knows that I am opposed on principle to the whole idea of marriage. That is what makes this woman's behavior so ridiculous. To think of getting *married* in a world that is in one of the most ghastly phases of its history is puerile."

He gave a short sarcastic laugh. The audience was indifferent.

The editor went into the telephone booth, and leaving the door open for all to hear, he rang her room.

"Julian Drood," he said brusquely. "It is important that I should see you at once, privately, in your room."

He heard her breathing. The way the human race thought it was enough if they breathed! Ask an important question and what happens? Breath. Then he heard the small voice: it made a splashing, confusing sound.

"Oh," it said. And more breath: "Yes."

The two words were the top of a wave that is about to topple and come thumping over onto the sand and then draws back with a long, insidious hiss.

"Please," she added. And the word was the long, thirsty hiss.

The editor was surprised that his brusque manner was so wistfully treated.

Good heavens, he thought, she *is* in that room! And because she was invisible and because of the distance of the wire between them, he felt she was pouring down it, head first, mouth open, swamping him. When he put the telephone down, he scratched his ear; a piece of her seemed to be coiled there. The editor's ear had heard passion. And passion at its climax.

He had often heard of passion. He had often been told of it. He had seen it in opera. He had friends—who usually came to him for advice—who were entangled in it. He had never felt it and he did not feel it now; but when he walked from the telephone booth to the lift, he saw his role had changed. The woman was not a mere nuisance—she was something out of *Tosca*. The pagan became doggish, the saint furtive as he entered the lift.

"Ah," the editor burst out aloud to the liftman, *"les femmes."* The German did not understand French.

The editor got out of the lift, and passing one watchful white door after another, came to 415. He knocked twice. When there was no answer he opened the door.

He seemed to blunder into an invisible wall of spice and scent and stepped back, thinking he had made a mistake. A long-legged rag doll with big blue eyes looked at him from the bed, a half-unpacked suitcase was on the floor with curious clothes hanging out of it. A woman's shoes were tipped out on the sofa.

And then, with her back to a small desk where she had been writing, stood Miss Mendoza. Or, rather, the bottle-green dress, the boxlike figure were Miss Mendoza's: the head was not. Her hair was no longer black: it was golden. The idol's head had been chopped off and was replaced by a woman's. There was no expression on the face until the shock on the editor's face passed to hers, then a searching look of horror seized her, then of one caught in an outrage. She lowered her head, cowed and frightened. She quickly grabbed a stocking she had left on the bed and held it behind her back.

"You are angry with me," she said, holding her head down like an obstinate child.

"You are in *my* room. You have no right to be here. I *am* very angry with you. What do you mean by registering in my name—apart from anything else, it is illegal.

You know that, don't you? I must ask you to go or I shall have to take steps . . ."

Her head was still lowered. Perhaps he ought not to have said the last sentence. The blond hair made her look pathetic.

"Why did you do this?"

"Because you would not see me," she said. "You have been cruel to me."

"But don't you realize, Miss Mendoza, what you are doing? I hardly know you. You have followed me all over Europe; you have badgered me. You take my room. You pretend to be my wife . . ."

"Do you hate me?" she muttered.

Damn, thought the editor. I ought to have changed my hotel at once.

"I know nothing about you," he said.

"Don't you want to know about me? What I am like? I know everything about you," she said, raising her head.

The editor was confused by the rebuke. His fit of acting passed. He looked at his watch.

"A reporter is coming to see me in half an hour," he said.

"I shall not be in the way," she said. "I will go out."

"*You* will go out!" said the editor.

Then he understood where he was wrong. He had forgotten—perhaps being abroad addressing meetings, speaking to audiences with only one mass face had done this—forgotten how to deal with difficult people.

He pushed the shoes to one end of the sofa to find himself a place. One shoe fell to the floor, but, after all, it was his room, he had a right to sit down.

"Miss Mendoza, you are ill," he said.

She looked down quickly at the carpet.

"I am not," she said.

"You are ill and, I think, very unhappy." He put on his wise voice.

"No," she said in a low voice. "Happy. You are talking to me."

"You are a very intelligent woman," he said. "And you will understand what I am going to say. Gifted people like yourself are very vulnerable. You live in the imagination, and that exposes one. I know that."

"Yes," she said. "You see all the injustices of the world. You bleed from them."

"I? Yes," said the editor with his saint's smile. But he recovered from the flattery. "I am saying something else. Your imagination is part of your gift as a poet, but in real life it has deluded you."

"It hasn't done that. I see you as you are."

"Please sit down," said the editor. He could not bear her standing over him. "Close the window, there is too much noise."

She obeyed. The editor was alarmed to see the zipper of her dress was half undone and he could see the top of some garment with ominous lace on it. He could not bear untidy women. He saw his case was urgent. He made a greater effort to be kind.

"It was very kind of you to come to my lectures. I hope you found them interesting. I think they went down all right—good questions. One never knows, of course. One arrives in a strange place and one sees a hall full of people one doesn't know—and you won't believe me perhaps because I've done it scores of times—but one likes to see a face that one recognizes. One feels lost, at first . . ."

She looked hopeful.

This was untrue. The editor never felt lost. Once on his feet he had the sensation that he was talking to the human race. He suffered with it. It was the general human suffering that had ravaged his face.

"But you know," he said sternly, "our feelings deceive us. Especially at certain times of life. I was worried about you. I saw that something was wrong. These things happen very suddenly. God knows why. You see someone whom you admire perhaps—it seems to happen to women more than men—and you project some forgotten love on him. You think you love him, but it is really some forgotten image. In your case, I would say, probably some image of your father whom you have hated all these years for what he did when you were a child. And so, as people say, one becomes obsessed or infatuated. I don't like the word. What we mean is that one is not in love with a real man or woman but a vision sent out by oneself. One can think of many examples . . ."

The editor was sweating. He wished he hadn't asked her to close the window. He knew his mind was drifting toward historic instances. He wondered if he would tell her the story of Jane Carlyle, the wife of the historian, who had gone to hear the famous Father Matthew speak at a temperance meeting and how, hysterical and exalted, she had rushed to the platform to kiss his boots. Or there were other instances. For the moment he couldn't remember them. He decided on Mrs. Carlyle. It was a mistake.

"Who is Mrs. Carlyle?" said Miss Mendoza suspiciously. "I would never kiss any man's feet."

"Boots," said the editor. "It was on a public platform."

"Or boots," Miss Mendoza burst out. "Why are you torturing me? You are saying I am mad."

The editor was surprised by the turn of the conversation. It had seemed to be going well.

"Of course you're not mad," he said. "A madwoman could not have written that great poem. I am just saying that I value your feeling, but you must understand that I, unfortunately, do not love you. But you *are* ill. You have exhausted yourself."

Miss Mendoza's yellow eyes became brilliant as she listened to him.

"So," she said grandly, "I am a mere nuisance."

She got up from her chair and he saw she was trembling.

"If that is so, why don't you leave this room at once?" she said.

"But," said the editor with a laugh, "if I may mention it, it is mine."

"I signed the register," said Miss Mendoza.

"Well," said the editor smiling, "that is not the point, is it?"

The boredom, the sense of the sheer waste of time (when one thought of the massacres, the bombings, the imprisonments in the world) in personal questions, overcame him. It amazed him that at some awful crisis—the Cuban, for example—how many people left their husbands, wives or lovers, in a general post: the extraordinary, irresponsible persistence of outbreaks of love. A kind of guerrilla war in another context. Here he was in the midst of it. What could he do? He looked around the room for help. The noise of the traffic outside in the street, the dim sight of people moving behind office windows opposite, an advertisement for beer were no help. Humanity had deserted him. The nearest thing to the human—now it took his eye—was the doll on the bed, an absurd marionette from the cabaret, the raffle or the nursery. It had a mop of red hair, silly red cheeks and popping blue eyes with long cotton lashes. It wore a short skirt and had long insane legs in checked stockings. How childish women were. Of course (it now occurred to him), Miss Mendoza was as childish as her voice. The editor said playfully, "I see you have a little friend. Very pretty. Does she come from Guatemala?" And frivolously, because he disliked the thing, he took a step or two toward it. Miss Mendoza pushed past him at once and grabbed it.

"Don't touch it," she said with tiny fierceness.

She picked up the doll, and hugging it with fear, she looked for somewhere to put it out of his reach. She went to the door, then changed her mind and rushed to the window with it. She opened the window, and as the curtains blew in, she looked as if a desperate idea had occurred to her—to throw herself and it out of the window. She turned to fight him off. He was too bewildered to move, and when she saw that he stood still her frightened face changed. Suddenly, she threw the doll on the floor, and half falling onto a chair near it, her shoulders rounded, she covered her face with her hands and sobbed, shaking her head from side to side. Tears crawled through her fingers down the backs of her hands. Then she took her hands away and, soft and shapeless, she rushed to the editor and clawed at his jacket.

"Go away. Go away," she cried. "Forgive me. Forgive. I'm sorry." She began to laugh and cry at once. "As you said—ill. Oh, please forgive. I don't understand why I did this. For a week I haven't eaten anything. I must have been out of my mind to do this to you. Why? I can't think. You've been so kind. You could have been cruel. You were right. You had the courage to tell me the truth. I feel so ashamed, so ashamed. What can I do?"

She was holding on to his jacket. Her tears were on his hands. She was pleading. She looked up.

"I've been such a fool," she said.

"Come and sit here," said the editor, trying to move her to the sofa. "You are not a fool. You have done nothing. There is nothing to be ashamed of."

"I can't bear it."

"Come and sit here," he said putting his arm on her shoulder. "I was very proud when I read your poem. Look," he said, "you are a very gifted and attractive woman."

He was surprised that such a heavy woman was not like

iron to the touch but light and soft. He could feel her
skin, hot through her dress. Her breath was hot. Agony
was hot. Grief was hot. Above all, her clothes were hot.
It was perhaps because of the heat of her clothes that for
the first time in years he had the sensation of holding a
human being. He had never felt this when, on a few
occasions, he had held a woman naked in her bed. He did
something then that was incredible to himself. He gently
kissed the top of her head on the blond hair he did not
like. It was like kissing a heated mat and it smelled of
burning.

At his kiss she clawed no longer and her tears stopped.
She moved away from him in awe.

"Thank you," she said gravely and he found himself
being studied, even memorized, as she had done when
she had first come to his office. The look of the idol was
set on her again. Then she uttered a revelation. "You do
not love anyone but yourself." And worse, she smiled.
He had thought, with dread, that she was waiting to be
kissed again, but now he couldn't bear what she said. It
was a loss.

"We must meet," he said recklessly. "We *shall* meet at
the lecture tonight."

The shadow of her future passed over her face.

"Oh no," she said. She was free. She was warning him
not to hope to exploit her pain.

"This afternoon?" he said trying to catch her hand,
but she drew it away. And then, to his bewilderment, she
was dodging round him. She was packing. She began
stuffing her few clothes into her suitcase. She went to the
bathroom, and while she was there the porter came in
with his two bags.

"Wait," said the editor.

She came out of the bathroom looking very pale and
put the remaining things into her suitcase.

"I asked him to wait," the editor said.

The kiss, the golden hair, the heat of her head, seemed to be flying round in the editor's head.

"I don't want you to leave like this," the editor said.

"I heard what you said to the man," she said hurriedly shutting the suitcase. "Good-bye. And thank you. You are saving me from something dreadful."

The editor could not move when he saw her go. He could not believe she had gone. He could feel the stir of her scent in the air, and he sat down exhausted but arguing with his conscience. Why had she said that about loving only himself? What else could he have done? He wished there were people there to whom he could explain, whom he could ask. He was feeling loneliness for one of the few times in his life. He went to the window to look down at the people. Then, looking back to the bed, he was astounded by a thought: I have never had an adventure in my life. And with that, he left the room and went down to the desk. Was she still in the hotel?

"No," said the desk clerk. "Mrs. Drood went off in a taxi."

"I am asking for Miss Mendoza."

"No one of that name."

"Extraordinary," lied the editor. "She was to meet me here."

"Perhaps she is at the Hofgarten—it's the same management."

For the next hour he was on the telephone, trying all the hotels. He got a cab to the station; he tried the airlines and then, in the afternoon, went out to the airport. He knew it was hopeless. I must be mad too, he thought. He looked at every golden-haired woman he could see—the city was full of golden-haired women. As the noisy city afternoon moved by, he gave up. He liked to talk about himself, but here was a day he could never describe to anyone. He could not return to his room but sat in the lounge trying to read a paper, wrangling with himself and looking up at every woman who passed. He could not eat or even drink, and when he went out to his lecture he walked all the way to the hall on the chance of seeing her. He had the fancy once or twice, which he laughed at bitterly, that she had just passed and had left two or three of her footprints on the pavement. The extraordinary thing was that she was exactly the kind of woman he could not bear: squat, ugly. How awful she must look without clothes on. He tried to exorcise her by obscene images. They vanished and some transformed idealized vision of her came back. He began to see her tall and dark or young and fair: her eyes changing color, her body voluptuously rounded, athletically slim. As he sat on the lecture platform, listening to the introduction, he made faces that astonished the audience with a mechanical display of eagerness followed by scorn as his gaze went systematically from row to row, looking for her. He got up to speak. "Ladies and gentlemen," he began. He knew it would be the best lecture he had ever given. It was. Urging, appealing, agonizing, eloquent. It was an appeal to her to come back.

And then, after a lot of discussion which he hardly heard, he returned to the hotel. He had now to face the mockery of the room. He let himself in and it did mock. The maid had turned the bed back and on it lay the doll, its legs tidied, its big ridiculous eyes staring at him. They seemed to him to blink. She had forgotten it. She had left her childhood behind.

Did You Invite Me?

RACHEL first met Gilbert at David and Sarah's, or it may have been at Richard and Phoebe's—she could not remember—but she did remember that he stood like a touchy exclamation mark and talked in a shotgun manner about his dog. His talk jumped, so that she got confused: the dog was his wife's dog but was he talking about his dog or his wife? He blinked very fast when he talked of either. Then she remembered what David (or maybe Richard) had told her. His wife was dead. Rachel had a dog, too, but Gilbert was not interested.

The bond between all of them was that they owned small white stuccoed houses, not quite alike—hers alone, for example, had Gothic churchy windows, which, she felt, gave her point—on different sides of the park. Another bond was that they had reached middle life and said nothing about it, except that Gilbert sharply pretended to be younger than the rest of them in order to remind them they had arrived at that time when one year passes into the next unnoticed, leaving among the dregs an insinuation that they had not done what they intended. When this thought struck them they would all— if they had the time—look out of their sedate windows at the park, the tame and once princely oasis where the trees looked womanish on the island in the lake or marched in grave married processions along the avenues in the late summer, or in the winter were starkly widowed. They could watch the weekend crowds or the solitary walkers on the public grass, see the duck flying over in the evenings, hear the keeper's whistle and his shout "All out!" when the gates of the Park closed an hour after sunset; and at night, hearing the animals at the zoo, they could send out silent cries of their own upon the place and evoke their ghosts.

But not Gilbert. His cry would be a howl and audible, a joint howl of himself and this dog he talked about. Rachel had never seen a man so howling naked. Something must be done about him, she thought every time she met him. Two years ago, Sonia, his famous and chancy wife, had died—"on the stage," the headlines in the London newspapers said, which was nearly true—and his eyes were red-rimmed as if she had died yesterday, his angry face was raw with drink or the unjust marks of guilt and grief. He was a tall man, all bones, and even his wrists coming out of a jacket that was too short in the sleeve seemed to be crying. He had also the look of a man who had decided not to buy another suit in his life, to let cloth go on gleaming with its private malice. It was well known—for he boasted of it himself—that his wife had been much older than he, that they had quarreled continually and that he still adored her.

Rachel had been naked, too, in her time when, six or seven years before, she had divorced her husband. Gilbert is "in the middle of it," she thought. She had been "through it" and had "come out of it," and was not hurt or lonely any more and had crowded her life with public troubles. She was married to a newspaper column.

"Something really *must* be done about him," she at last said out loud to David and Sarah as she tried to follow Gilbert's conversation that was full of traps and false exit lines. For his part, he sniffed when he spoke to them of Rachel.

"Very attractive woman. Very boring. All women are
boring. Sonia was a terrible bore sometimes, carrying
on, silly cow. What of it? You may have remarked it: I'm
a bore. I must go. Thank you, Sarah and David, for
inviting me and offering me your friendship. You did
invite me, didn't you? You did? I'm glad. I have no
friends. The friends Sonia and I invited to the house
were hers, not mine. Old codgers. I must go home and
feed her dog."

They watched him go off stiffly, a forty-year-old.

An outsider he was, of course, because of loss. One
feels the east wind—she knew that. But it was clear—as
she decided to add him to her worries—that he must
always have been that. He behaved mechanically, *click,
click, click,* like a puppet or an orphan, homelessness being his vanity. This came out when David had asked
Gilbert about his father and mother in her presence.
From David's glances at his wife, Rachel knew they had
heard what he said many times before. Out came his
shot, the long lashes of his childish eyes blinking fast:
"Never met the people."

He was showing contempt for a wound. He was born
in Singapore, he said. One gathered the birth had no
connection with either father or mother. She tried to be
intelligent about the city.

"Never saw the place," he said. The father became a
prisoner of the Japanese: the mother took him to India.
Rachel tried to be intelligent about India.

"Don't remember it," he said.

"The old girl," his mother, sent him home to schools
and holiday schools. He spent his boyhood in camps and
dormitories, his army life in Nissen huts. He was twenty
when he really "met" his parents. At the sight of him
they separated for good.

No further answers. Life had been doled out to him
like spoonfuls of medicine, one at a time; he returned the
compliment by doing the same and then erected silences

like packs of cards, watching people wait for them to fall down.

How, Rachel asked, did the raw young man come to be married to Sonia, an actress at the top of the tree, fifteen years older than he? "The old girl knew her," he said; she was his mother's friend. Rachel worried away at it. She saw, correctly, a dramatic woman with a clever mouth, a surrogate mother—but a mother astute in acting the part among her scores of grand and famous friends. Rachel had one or two famous friends too, but he snubbed her with his automatic phrase: "Never met him." Or: "Never met her."

And then Rachel, again correctly, saw him standing in the doorway of Sonia's drawing room or bringing drinks perhaps to the crowd, like an uncouth son; those wrists were the wrists of a growing boy who silently jeered at the guests. She heard Sonia dressing him down for his Nissen-hut language and his bad manners—which, however, she encouraged. This was her third marriage and it had to be original. That was the heart of the Gilbert problem: Sonia had invented him; he had no innate right to be what he appeared to be.

So Rachel, who happened to be writing an article on broken homes, asked him to come round and have a drink. He walked across the park from his house to hers. At the door he spoke his usual phrase, "Thank you for inviting me. You did invite me, didn't you? Well, I thank you. We live on opposite sides of the park. Very convenient. Not too near."

He came in.

"Your house is white and your dog is white," he said.

Rachel owned a dog. A very white fox terrier came barking at him on a high, glassy note, showing a ratter's teeth. Rachel was wearing a long pale-blue dress from her throat to the tips of her shoes and led him into the sitting room. He sank into a soft silky sofa with his knees

together and politely inspected her as an interesting collection of bones.

"Shall I ever get up from this?" he said, patting the
sofa. "Silly question. Yes, I shall, of course. I have come,
shortly I shall go." He was mocking someone's manners.
Perhaps hers. The fox terrier, which had followed him
into the small and sunny room, sniffed long at Gilbert's
shoes and his trouser legs and stiffened when he stroked
its head. The dog growled.

"Pretty head," he said. "I like dogs' heads." He was
staring at Rachel's head. Her hair was smooth, neat and
fair.

"I remarked his feet on the hall floor, tick, tick, tick.
Your hall must be tiled. Mine is carpeted."

"Don't be so aggressive, Sam," said Rachel gravely to
the dog.

"Leave him alone," said Gilbert. "He can smell Tom,
Sonia's bull terrier. That's who you can smell, isn't it? He
can smell an enemy."

"Sam is a problem," she said. "Everyone in the street
hates you, Sam, don't they? When you get out in the
garden you bark and bark, people open their windows
and shout at you. You chase cats, you killed the Gregory
boy's rabbit and bit the Jackson child. You drive the
doctor mad. He throws flower pots at you."

"Stop nagging the poor animal," said Gilbert. And to
the dog he said, "Good for you. Be a nuisance. Be yourself. Everyone needs an enemy. Absolutely."

And he said to himself, She hasn't forgiven her husband. In her long dress she had the composure of the
completely smoothed-over person who might well have
nothing on underneath. Gilbert appreciated this, but she
became prudish and argumentative.

"Why do you say 'absolutely,' " she said, seeing a dis-
tracting point for discussion here. "Isn't that relative?"

"No," said Gilbert with enjoyment. He loved a row.

"I've got an enemy at my office. Nasty little creepy fellow. He wants my job. He watches me. There's a new job
going—promotion—and he thinks I want it. So he
watches. He sits on the other side of the room and is
peeing himself with anxiety every time I move. Peeing
himself, yes. If I leave the room he goes to the door to
see if I'm going to the Director's office. If I do he sweats.
He makes an excuse to go to the Director to see if he can
find out what we've been talking about. When I am working on a scheme he comes over to look at it. If I'm
working out costs he stares with agony at the layout and
the figures. 'Is that Jameson's?' He can't contain himself.
'No, I'm doing my income tax,' I tell him. He's very
shocked at my doing that in office hours and goes away
relieved. He'll report that to the Director. Then a suspicion strikes him when he is halfway back to his desk and
he turns round and comes over again panting. He
doesn't believe me. 'I'm turning inches into centime-
ters,' I say. He still doesn't believe me. Poor silly bug-
ger." He laughed.

"Wasn't that rather cruel?" she said. "Why centime-
ters?"

"Why not? He wants the French job. Boring little man.
Boring office. Yes."

Gilbert constructed one of his long silences. Rachel
saw skyscrapers, pagodas, the Eiffel Tower and this little
man creeping up them like an ant. After a while Gilbert
went on and the vision collapsed. "He was the only one
who came from the office to Sonia's funeral. He brought
his wife—never met her before—and she cried. The only
person who did. Yes. He'd never missed a show Sonia
was in."

"So he isn't an enemy. Doesn't that prove my point?"
she said solemnly. Gilbert ignored this.

"They'd never met poor Sonia," he said. And he
blinked very fast.

"I never met your wife either, you know," said Rachel earnestly. She hoped he would describe her; but he described her doctors, the lawyers that assemble after death.

"What a farce," he said. "She had a stroke in the theater. Her words came out backwards. I wrote to her two husbands. Only one replied. The theater sent her to hospital in an ambulance—the damn fools. If you go to hospital you die of pneumonia, bloody hospital won't give you enough pillows, you lie flat and you can't get your breath. What a farce. Her brother came and talked, one of those fat men. Never liked the fellow."

She said how terrible it must have been. "Did she recover her speech? They sometimes do."

"Asked," he said, "for the dog. Called it God."

He got up suddenly from the sofa.

"There! I have got up. I am standing on my feet. I am a bore," he said. "I shall go."

As he left the room the terrier came sniffing at his heels.

"Country dogs. Good ratters. Ought to be on a farm."

She plunged into a confidence to make him stay longer.

"He used to be a country dog. My husband bought him for me when we lived in the country. I know"—she luxuriated in a worry—"how important environment is to animals and I was going to let him stay, but when you are living alone in a city like London—well—there are a lot of burglaries here."

"Why did you divorce your husband?" he asked as he opened the front door. "I shouldn't have asked. Bad manners. I apologize. I was rude. Sonia was always on to me about that."

"He went off with a girl at his office," she said staunchly.

"Silly man," said Gilbert, looking at the dog. "Thank

you. Good-bye. Do we shake hands? You invited me, now
it is my turn to invite you. That is the right thing, of
course it is. We must do the right thing. I shall."

Weeks passed before Gilbert invited Rachel. There
were difficulties. Whatever he decided by day was de-
stroyed at night. At night Sonia would seem to come
flying out of the park saying the house had belonged to
her. She had paid for it. She enumerated the furniture
item by item. She had the slow, languid walk of her stage
appearances as she went suspiciously from room to
room, asking what he had done with her fur coats and
where her shoes were. "You've given them to some
woman." She said he had a woman in the house. He said
he asked only David and Sarah; she said she didn't trust
Sarah. He pleaded he had kept the dog. When he said
that, her ghost vanished saying he starved the poor
thing. One night he said to her, "I'm going to ask Rachel,
but you'll be there." "I damn well will," she said. And
this became such a dogma that when, at last, he asked
Rachel to come, he disliked her.

His house was not as sedate as hers, which had been
repainted that year—his not. His windows seemed to him
—and to her—to sob. There was grit on the frames.
When he opened the door to her she noted the brass
knocker had not been polished and inside there was the
immediate cold odor of old food. The hall and walls
echoed their voices and the air was very still. In the
sitting room the seats of the chairs, one could see, had
not been sat on for a long time, there was dust on the
theatrical wallpaper. Hearing her, Sonia's dog, Tom,
came scrabbling the stair carpet and rushed into the
room hysterically at both of them, skidding on rugs,
snuffling, snorting, whimpering and made at once for
her skirts, got under her legs and was driven off onto a
sofa of green silk, rather like hers, but now frayed where
the dog's claws had caught.

"Off the sofa, Tom," said Gilbert. The dog ignored this and snuffled from its squat nose and gazed from wet eyes that were like enormous marbles. Gilbert picked up a rubber bone and threw it to the dog. Down it came and the racing round the room began again. Rachel held her glass in the air for safety's sake and the dog jumped at it and made her spill whiskey on her dress. In this confusion they tried to talk.

"Sonia liked being photographed with Tom," he said.

"I only saw her on the stage once. She was very beautiful," she said. "It must have been twelve years ago. Gielgud and another actor called Slade were in it. Was it Slade? Oh dear! My memory!"

"Her second husband," he said.

He picked up the dog's rubber bone. The dog rushed to him and seized it. Man and dog pulled at the bone.

"You want it. You won't get it," said Gilbert while she seemed to hear her husband say: "Why can't you keep your mouth shut if you can't remember things?" And Gilbert, grinning in his struggle with the dog, said, "Sonia always had Tom to sleep on our bed. He still does. Won't leave it. He's on it even when I come back from the office."

"He sleeps with you?" she said with a shudder.

"I come home. I want someone to talk to."

"What d'you do with him when you go to your office?" The dog pulled and snorted.

"The woman who comes in and cleans looks after the dog," he said. And went on: "Your house has three stories, mine has two, otherwise the same. I've got a basement full of rubbish. I was going to turn it into a flat but Sonia got worse. Futile. Yes, life is futile. Why not sell the damn place. No point. No point in anything. I go to the office, come back, feed the dog and get drunk. Why not? Why go on? Why do *you* go on? Just habit. No sense in it."

"You *do* go on," she said.

"The dog," he said.

I must find some people for him to meet. He can't live like this, she thought. It is ghastly.

When she left he stood on the doorstep and said, "My house. Your house. They're worth four times what we gave for them. There it is."

She decided to invite him to dinner to meet some people—but whom could she ask? He was prickly. She knew dozens of people, but as she thought of them there seemed, for the first time, to be something wrong with all of them. In the end she invited no one to meet him.

On a diet, silly cow, he thought when she came to the door, but he fell back on his usual phrase as he looked about the empty room. "Did you invite me? Or shall I go away? You *did* invite me. Thank you. Thank you."

"I've been in Vienna with the Fladgates. She is a singer. Friends of David and Sarah."

"Fladgates? Never heard of the people," he said. "Sonia insulted someone in Vienna. I was drunk. Sonia never drank anything—that made her insults worse. Did your husband drink?"

"Indeed not."

He sat down on the sofa. The evening—Sonia's time. He expected Sonia to fly in and sit there watching this woman with all her "problems" hidden chastely except for one foot which tipped up and down in her shoe under her long dress. But—to his surprise—Sonia did not come. The terrier sat at Rachel's feet.

"How is your enemy?" she said as they drank. "The man in the office."

"He and his wife asked me to dinner," he said.

"That's kind," she said.

"People are kind," he said. "I've remarked that."

"Does he still watch you?"

"Yes. You know what it was? He thinks I drink too much. He thinks I've got a bottle in my desk. It wasn't the job that was worrying him. We are wrong about people. I am. You are. Everyone is."

When they went into dinner, candles were on the table.

Bloody silly having candles, he said to himself. And when she came in with the soup, he said, "We had candles. Poor Sonia threw them out of the window once. She had to do it in a play."

The soup was iced and white and there was something in it that he could not make out. But no salt. That's it, he thought, no salt in this woman. Writing about politics and things all day and forgets the salt. The next course was white too, something chopped or minced with something peculiar, goodness knew what. It got into his teeth. Minced newsprint, he thought.

"Poor Sonia couldn't cook at all," he said, pushing his food about, proud of Sonia. "She put dishes on the floor near the stove, terrible muddle and rushed back to hear what people were saying and then an awful bloody stink came from the kitchen. I used to go down and the potatoes had burned dry and Tom had cleared the plates. Bloody starvation. No dinner."

"Oh no!" she said.

"I live on chops now. Yes," he said. "One, sometimes two, every day, say ten a week. Am I being a bore? Shall I go?"

Rachel had a face that had been set for years in the same concerned expression. That expression now fell to pieces from her forehead to her throat. Against her will she laughed. The laugh shook her and was loud; she felt herself being whirled into a helpless state from the toes upward. Her blood whirled too.

"You laughed!" he shouted. "You did not protest. You did not write an article. You laughed. I could see your teeth. Very good. I've never seen you laugh before."

And the dog barked at them.

"She laughed," he shouted at the dog.

She went out to make coffee, very annoyed at being trapped into laughing. While he waited, the dog sat undecided, ears pricked, listening for her and watching him like a sentry.

"Rats," whispered Gilbert to the dog. It stood up sharply.

"Poor bastard. What a life," he said.

The dog barked angrily at him, and when she came in he said, "I told your dog he ought to be on a farm."

"You said that before," she said. "Let us have coffee next door." They moved into the next room and she sat on the sofa while she poured the coffee.

"Now *you* are sitting on the sofa. I'm in this armchair," he said, thinking of life tactically. "Sonia moved about too. I used to watch her going into a room. Where will she sit next? Damned if I ever got it right. The same in restaurants. Let us sit here, she'd say, and then when the waiter came to her chair, she'd say, 'No, not here. Over there.' Never knew where she was going to settle. Like a fly. She wanted attention. Of course. That was it. Quite right."

"Well," she said coldly, "she was an actress."

"Nothing to do with it," he said. "Woman."

"Nonsense," she said, hating to be called a woman, and thought, It's my turn now.

"My husband," she said, "traveled the whole time. Moscow, Germany, Copenhagen, South Africa, but when he got home he was never still, posing to the animals on the farm, showing off to barns, fences, talking French and German to birds, pretending to be a country gentleman."

"Let the poor man alone," he said. "Is he still alive?"

"I told you," she said. "I won't bore you with it all."

She was astonished to find herself using his word and that the full story of her husband and herself she had planned to tell and which she had told so many people suddenly lost interest for her. And yet, anyway, she thought, why shouldn't I tell this man about it? So she started, but she made a muddle of it. She got lost in the details. The evening, she saw, was a failure. He yawned.

If there was one thing Rachel could honestly say, it was that she had not thought of her husband for years. She had not forgotten, but he had become a generality in the busyness of her life. But now, after the evening when Gilbert came to dinner, her husband came to life and plagued her. If an airplane came down whistling across the wide London sky, she saw him sitting in it—back from Moscow, Capetown, Copenhagen—descending not upon her, but on another woman. If she took the dog for a run in the park, the cuddling couples on the grass became him and that young girl; if babies screamed in their prams they were his children; if a man threw a ball it was he; if men in white flannels were playing cricket, she wondered if he was among them. She imagined sudden, cold meetings and ran through tirades of hot dialogue. One day she saw a procession of dogs tails up and panting, following a bitch, with a foolish grin of wet teeth in their jaws and Sam rushed after them; she went red in the face shouting at him. And yet she had gone to the park in order to calm herself and to be alone. The worst thing that could happen would be to meet Gilbert, the cause of this, but like all malevolent causes, he never showed his face. She had wished to do her duty and be sorry for him, but not for him to become a man. She feared she might be on the point of talking about this to a woman, not a woman she knew well—that would be disastrous—but, say, to some woman or girl sitting alone on a park seat or some woman in a shop: a confidence she would regret all her life. She was touchy in these days and had a row with the doctor who threw flower pots at her dog. She petted the animal. "Your head is handsome," she said, stroking its head, "but why did you go after that silly bitch?" The dog adored her when she said this. "You're vain," she said to it.

Gilbert *did* go to the park but only on Saturdays when the crowds came. He liked seeing the picnics, the litter on the grass; he stood still with pleasure when babies screamed or ice cream dripped. He grinned at boys throwing water from drinking fountains and families trudging, drunks lying asleep, and fat girls lying half on top of their young men and tickling their faces with grass. The place is a damn bedroom. Why not? Where else can they go? Lucky, boring people. I've got a bedroom and no on in it.

One Saturday, after three days of rain, he took his dog there and—would you believe it?—there the whole crowd was again, still at it, on the wet grass. The trouble with Sonia was that she thought the park was vulgar and would never go there—went once and never again, hadn't brought the right shoes.

He remarked this to his dog as he let it off its leash. The animal scampered round him in wide circles; came back to him and then raced off again in circles getting wider and wider, until it saw a man with string in his hand trying to fly a kite. The kite was flopping on the ground, rose twenty or thirty feet in the air and then dived again. The dog rushed at the kite, but the man got it up again, higher this time. Gilbert walked toward the man. "Poor devil, can't get it up," he said as he walked. He got near the man and watched his struggles.

Then the kite shot up high and Gilbert watched it raving there until suddenly it swept away higher still. Gilbert said, "Good for him." The boredom of the gray afternoon was sweet. He lit a cigarette and threw the empty packet on the grass and then he found he had lost sight of the dog. When he saw it again it was racing in a straight line toward a group of trees by the lake. It was racing toward another dog. A few yards away from the dog it stopped and pranced. The dog was a terrier and stopped dead, then came forward. They stood sniffing at each other's tails and then jumped round muzzle to muzzle. They were growling, the terrier barked, and then the two dogs flew at each other's necks. Their play had turned to a war, their jaws were at each other's necks and ears. Gilbert saw at once it was Rachel's dog, indeed Rachel was running up shouting, "Sam! Sam!" The fight was savage and Tom had his teeth in.

"Stop them!" Rachel was shouting. "Stop them! They'll kill each other. He's got him by the throat."

And then she saw Gilbert. "You!"

Gilbert was enjoying the fight. He looked around and picked up a stick that had fallen from a tree.

"Stop them," she shouted.

"Get yours by the collar, I'll get mine," he shouted to her.

"I can't. Sam! Sam! They're bleeding."

She was dancing about in terror, trying to catch Sam by the legs.

"Not by the legs. By the collar, like this, woman," he shouted. "Don't put your arms round him, you idiot. Like this. Stop dancing about."

He caught Tom by the collar and lifted him as both dogs hung on to each other.

"You're strangling him. I can't, I can't," she said. Gilbert brought his stick down hard on the muzzles of the dogs, just as she was trying to grasp Sam again.

"You'll kill them."

He brought the stick down hard again. The dogs yelped with pain and separated.

"Get the leash on," he said, "you fool."

Somehow she managed it and the two dogs now strained to get at each other. The terrier's white neck and body were spotted with blood, and smears of it were on her hands.

Gilbert wiped their spit off his sleeve.

They pulled their dogs yards apart and she stared at him. It infuriated her that he was laughing at her with pure pleasure. In their stares they saw each other clearly and as they had never seen each other before. To him, in her short skirt and her shoes muddied by the wet grass, her hair disordered and the blood risen to her pale face, she was a woman. The grass had changed her. To her he was not a pitiable arrangement of widower's tricks, but a man on his own. And the park itself changed him in her eyes: in the park he, like everyone else there, seemed to be human. The dogs gave one more heave to get at each other.

"Lie down, Sam," Gilbert shouted.

She lifted her chin and was free to hate him for shouting at her animal.

"Look after yours. He's dangerous," she called back, angered by the friendliness of his face.

"Damn silly dogs enjoyed it. Good for them. Are you all right? Go up to the kiosk and get a drink—if I may, I'll follow you up—see you're all right."

"No, no," she put out a loud moan—far too loud. "He's bleeding. I'll take him home," and she turned to look at the park. "What a mess people make." And now, walking away, shouted a final accusation: "I didn't know you brought your dog here."

He watched her go. She turned away and dragged the struggling terrier over the grass uphill from the lake. He watched her walking unsteadily.

Very attractive figure, he thought. Silly cow. Better go home and ring her up.

He turned and on the way back to his house he could still see her dancing about on the grass and shouting. He went over the scene again and repeated his conclusion. "She's got legs. Never saw them before. A woman. Must be. Full of life." She was still dancing about as he put a bowl of water down for the dog. It drank noisily and he gave it another bowl and then he washed the dog's neck and looked at its ear. "Nothing much wrong with you," he said. He fed the animal, and soon it jumped on the sofa and was instantly snorting, whimpering and shaking into sleep.

"I must ring her up, yes, that is what I must do."

But a neighbor answered and said Rachel had gone to the vet and had come back in a terrible state and had gone to bed with one of her migraines.

"Don't bother her," he said. "I just rang to ask how the dog was."

Rachel was not in bed. She was standing beside the neighbor, and when the call was over she said, "What did he say?"

"He asked about the dog."

"Is that all?"

"Yes."

This flabbergasted her.

In the middle of the night she woke up, and when her stupefaction passed she damn well wished he was there so that she could say, "It didn't occur to you to apologize. I don't like being called a fool. You assume too much. Don't think I care a damn about *your* dog." She was annoyed to feel a shudder pass through her. She got out of bed, and looking out of her window at the black trees, saw herself racing across the park to his house and pulling that dog of his off his bed. The things she said! The language she used! She kicked the dog out of the room and it went howling downstairs. She went back to bed weak and surprised at herself because, before she realized it, Sam became Tom in her hand. She lay there stiff, awake, alone. Which dog had she kicked? Sam or Tom?

In his house Gilbert locked up, poured himself a strong whiskey, then a second, then a third. Uncertain of whom he was addressing, Rachel or Sonia, he said, "Silly cow," and blundered drunkish to bed. He woke up at five very cold. No dog. The bed was empty. He got out of bed and went downstairs. For the first time since Sonia had died the dog was asleep on the sofa. He had forgotten to leave his door open.

In the morning he was startled to hear Sonia's voice saying to him in her stage voice, "Send her some flowers. Ask her to dinner."

So he sent the flowers, and when Rachel rang to thank him he asked her to dinner—at a restaurant.

"Your house. My house," he said. "Two dogs."

There was a long silence and he could hear her breath bristling.

"Yes, I think it has to be somewhere else," she said. And added, "As you say, we have a problem."

And after this dinner and the next, she said, "There are so many problems. I don't really know you."

They talked all summer, and people who came regularly to the restaurant made up stories about them and were quite put out when in October they stopped coming. All the proprietor had heard was that they had sold their houses—in fact, he knew what they'd got for them. The proprietor had bought Sonia's dog. There was a terrier, too, he said, but he didn't know what had happened to that.

The Last Throw

T H E new week began for Karvo. For him weeks were always new. Cheered by the doorman, receptionists, secretaries, he went impatiently into purdah in the lift: on the silent top floor he came out, all animal, onto the stretches of green carpet which seemed to grow like the lawns of the country-house life he had just left. He raced to his enormous desk, on which lay an elephant's foot mounted on silver presented to him by an African ruler after his latest film, and he pressed a button. The call was answered by the fit of dry coughing that contained Chatterton.

"Chatty," Karvo began vigorously—then reproachfully, "I thought you had given up smoking?"

"I have," said Chatty. "That was nostalgia. I live in the past."

"Can you spare a minute?"

It always took Chatty longer to get to Karvo than Karvo could bear. Passing the open doors of offices, meeting people in the corridors, anywhere in the building, Chatty paused and, with the cough and the ravaged smile of dandyish human wreckage, asked people how they were. How far downhill on the way to dilapidation are you, when shall we all be human souls together? his large eyes seemed to ask. One or two hypochondriacs would tell him in detail. Why does this preposterous

organization run so well, Chatty sometimes asked himself—for he had the vanity of casualties—and replied, "I
am the oil in the wheels, the perambulating clinic, the
ambulance, the Salvation Army, the conscience—if it has
one—kept alive by a sun lamp, an expensive tailor and
dozens of teeny-weeny little pills." And with the air of
one saying Good-bye to himself, Chatty walked on.

Also, he added honestly, kept alive by Karvo, King of
Kings, the Elephant's Foot, the Life Force. Now for the
Monday morning shot! At board meetings Chatty often
doodled pictures of Karvo as an elephant sitting in the
studio with a crown on his head, a cigar in his mouth and
a scepter in his hand, while a naked cast of well-known
actors and actresses and teams of cameramen the size of
ants crawled before him. Now Chatty slipped into Karvo's room like a well-dressed fever and saw Karvo in
clothes that Karvo supposed were the right thing for
high life in the English countryside. He was sitting in
front of a very fat book that looked like the family Bible
and there was an uncommon expression of piety or, at
any rate, of elevation on his large, unmanageable face.

"When did you go to the doctor last?" said Karvo
kindly, but passed immediately to what he loved to talk
about on Mondays: his weekend.

Karvo was at that period in his life when the tide of
democracy and cinema had floated him into the private
boscage where peers, millionaires and merchant bankers
spent their lives. Chatty sat down on a sofa and waited
to be carried into Karvo's dreamland. At once Karvo was
on to the Hamilton-Spruces for a second, advanced to
the Hollinsheds and then, after a long detour among the
connections of the Esterhazys, the Radziwills, the
Hohenzollerns, the Hotspurs, Talbots, Buckinghams,
the Shakespearean cast of the English counties, finally
swerved to France to meet the Albigenses.

"Aren't they cousins of the Radziwills?" Karvo wanted
to know.

"No," said Chatty. "The Albigenses were a persecuted race. They are extinct."

Karvo turned to the title page of the book before him. It was not the Bible: it was not the *Almanach de Gotha*. It was a bound typescript.

"They were massacred," said Chatty. "In the South of France. About the twelfth century. Because of their religion."

"The South of France," said Karvo. His eyes switched on a sharp commercial light. "How many were massacred?"

He was thinking of a crowd scene.

"I don't know—a million; no, perhaps only a few hundred thousand," said Chatty.

"The French ambassador gave this manuscript to me at the Hamilton-Spruces. His wife wrote it," said Karvo. "Will you have a look at it?" Chatty had one more of his coughing fits as he took the manuscript.

"You *haven't* given up," Karvo accused him. "Cheating never pays."

"It's your cigar," said Chatty.

Chatty went to his office, opened the bottom drawer of the desk where he kept his dozens of bottles of pills and rested his feet on the open drawer as he sat down to read. First he looked up the name of the ambassador. Then he studied the name on the title page. As he expected, the author could not possibly be the wife of the French ambassador. In the hothouse of Society, Karvo usually misnamed the blooms. The name of that lady was not even in the long list of acknowledgments which began with a few eminences, went on to the Bibliothèque Nationale, the British Museum, combed the universities, and ended with inexhaustible gratitude to a dearest husband without whose constant advice and patient etc., etc. The dedication read, "To Doggie from Pussy."

Chatty studied the index and appendices and then, rearranging his feet on the drawer, was unable to prevent himself from memorizing six hundred pages of historical research. On Friday he went in to see Karvo.

"I'm just off to the country," he said. "I've read that thing. The author is Christine Johnson, a learned woman, first-class historian—no doubt about that. If you're interested in the Albigenses, this is the last word. You'll be glad to hear about the Cathari heresy. You know, of course, that the Cathari were dualists. Early dieters too: fast Monday, Wednesday and Friday every week. This annoyed the Pope. I think she'll have trouble all the same in Chapters Nine and Ten. Speaking as an historian . . ."

Karvo looked up from the script he was reading.

"Thank you," said Chatty. "Speaking as an historian I would say she is entirely speculative in Chapter Ten. Mad, I'd say. Massacres, of course. Several. The Albigenses were exterminated. There's nothing in it for us."

"Massacres?" said Karvo again. "What's the story?"

"Page 337. Incest," said Chatty. "Brother and sister, separated at birth by religious fanatics, meet again, don't know each other, get married—not knowing that after she's been raped in Toulouse and as they escape over the Pyrenees a woman called Clothilde de San Severino has betrayed them to the Inquisition, which tortures both. Roughly that."

"Torture," said Karvo looking up. "What kind? Incest? Have you marked the pages I'd like to see?" He softened. "My sister would never have let you get into the state you're in, Chatty. Would you mind seeing this woman—just politeness—tact, you know."

"All right," said Chatty.

Karvo's face blurred into one of his occasional looks of shame.

"Do you know her?" Chatty said.
Karvo shrugged.

The woman, Christine Johnson, had gone to her house in Paris but came to Chatty's office a fortnight later. Chatty spent an hour and a half with her. Late in the afternoon he went to Karvo's office, opening the door wide instead of sliding in, and shutting it with careful ceremony. He sat down on Karvo's distant sofa, put his feet up and said nothing.

"You're quiet," said Karvo.

"Have you ever experienced a miracle?" said Chatty.

"Many," said Karvo.

"Yes, I know. So have I. I'll put it another way. Have you ever met again or accidentally passed in the street, your first girl friend whom you haven't seen or heard of for fifteen or twenty years?"

"Mine was in my pram," said Karvo. "I don't remember."

"I'm not talking of childish vice. I mean your first adult girl friend. Have you seen her since, even at a distance?"

"That's a miracle I've avoided."

"Why?" said Chatty. "I can see her: short, very fat, strong glasses, a touch of something on the skin, spots perhaps, dirty raincoat, sullen with congested virtue, round-shouldered. (There's nothing against that. A lot of girls go in for being round-shouldered: they are trying out ways of being important or graceful, learning the job.) But wearing a seaman's heavy black jersey, no breasts or, rather, creased woolen bumps. The jersey is too large. Walking as if still marching into the classroom. 'Girls! Forward, march! Follow Diana.' Another thing—you could never see her alone. She was always with some other girl—very pretty, but for some insane reason the pretty one didn't appeal to you."

"Come to the point," said Karvo.

"And I don't suppose you've ever seen her years later with the man she married eventually. You imagined he was a weed who kept a small electrical shop or something like that and they lived out at—well, you know those places—with four children who have kicked the garden to pieces. Informative, rebuking, that's what she was. Always ticking you off—'No, Karvo. Stop it, Karvo.'"

"I remember that," said Karvo, putting on his martyred face. "Stop wasting my time. Kitchen sink is finished in pictures—you know that, Chatty."

"I've just met mine," said Chatty. "Can I have a drink? No, don't ring for it. I'll get it myself."

Chatty went to Karvo's drink cabinet. It was large and designed to look like the west front of a Gothic cathedral but without the saints.

"I can see why you shy off the subject," said Chatty. "I would have done so two hours ago, until Christine walked into my office. Except for the electrician and the four children, she used to be exactly as I have told you —but, my God! A butterfly has risen from that awful chrysalis. If it had been her pretty friend Ann I would not have been surprised—but Christine! The miracle has happened. As a matter of fact, I must have changed too. Down at reception she told the girl she had an appointment with Sir Arthur Chatterton. She is not the wife of the French ambassador."

"Who said she was?" said Karvo.

"Sweet Jesus—but let it pass.

"She's not only exquisite. She has brains." Chatty's voice became sad. "More than brains. Considering what she's got—what a waste."

"How d'you mean?" said Karvo. "Many women have first-class minds."

"I wasn't thinking of her mind," said Chatty. "I was thinking of her money. She's rich. I was thinking of her clothes. How many distinguished lady historians do you know with emeralds on their fingers, who have sacked Paris for their clothes, whose hats seem to have blown over from the Place Vendôme and who, besides owning houses in London and Paris, spend their winters on their dear, dear brother's estate in Toulouse?

"She was wearing a hat like a birthday cake made of air and a very short dress. I suppose it was a dress? She seemed to be getting out of it rather than wearing it— pretty well succeeded on the left thigh and the right shoulder. A hothouse flower with large glasses like windows. All the fat gone. A butterfly—but what am I talking about? A dragonfly," he said. He coughed.

"You oughtn't to talk so much," said Karvo.

"I knew her by her teeth," Chatty said sadly. "And her voice. It used to come out frosted out of the heart's deep freeze. It still does. Oh dear, it brought it all back. Christine and then her pretty friend Ann and me all sitting in Lipps," said Chatty.

"Is she married?" said Karvo.

"To a man in the Foreign Office, an adviser, whatever that is. Ronnie," said Chatty.

"So," said Karvo. "You've missed the boat."

"Oh no," said Chatty, "they've asked me to dinner the week after next when they come back from Scotland. They're staying with the Loch Lomonds."

Karvo raised both his chins.

"I've stayed with the Loch Lomonds," he said.

"So what was it like?" Karvo sneered. "Bollinger, Mouton Rothschild . . ."

Chatty was lying once more on the sofa in Karvo's room.

"You remember the husband of your first girl friend," said Chatty. "The man with the small electrical shop or television rentals, if you like—the man who replaced you in the loving heart you broke . . ."

"I never broke any girl's heart," said Karvo, looking up from his letters. "Accountants break mine."

"Imagine you are back in Paris. Now here's a girl, Cambridge, double first, ruins her poor pink-rimmed eyes in the Bibliothèque Nationale, borrows the occasional ten or twenty francs from you because she's hungry—you see her, this Miss Sorbonne in her chrysalis days, your friend, suddenly avoiding you in the Boulevard Saint Germain, walking by night, in silence, except that she scrapes a foot. She is with a tall young man who keeps bumping his dirty raincoat into hers because he walks aslant and bends to talk down into the top of her head, as if he were trying to graze there—not that there was much to graze on, her hair was very thin. He edges her towards the gutter or into those walls saying *Défense d'afficher,* as the case may be, talking about the Guermantes, say . . . And you say bitterly to yourself, 'Two pairs of strong glasses, two sets of rabbit teeth have felt an irresistible attraction.' "

One of Karvo's telephones rang.

"Karvo," said Karvo, heaving half of his body over the desk and in a voice suddenly plaintive said, "No, my darling. Yes, my darling. You'd better not, my darling. In that case you must, my darling."

And then put down the telephone and got his body back onto the chair, breathless, his eyelids blinking, paler than his face. He had his crucifixion look and he said to Chatty, "What were you saying? That was Dolly."

"I was saying," said Chatty, sitting up and raising his voice, "they now live in a bloody mansion! Cézannes, Picassos, Soutines, Renoirs, up the stairs, everywhere. From the drawing-room window you can see all the most expensive flowering shrubs and trees in bloom in the Crescent. A manservant brings in the champagne and in comes the adviser to the Foreign Office."

"Who is that?"

"I've told you," said Chatty. "Ronnie.

"There he is," said Chatty. "And he leans down and starts grazing on *your* hair now. He is young but has gone bald early—very confidential and nods at every word you say. Congratulating himself. As she floats into the room he says, 'It's a winner, isn't it?'

"She is wearing a dress made of two sheets of flame. One of the flames appears to be looped between her legs, but, of course, that can't be true, and for the rest of the evening you keep trying to work out how she got it on. And she says, as she comes in, 'Doggie!' And he looks at her and says 'Pussy!' They've come back from Scotland via Vienna and Paris."

"Who else was at the party?" said Karvo thirstily.

"No party," said Chatty. "Just his sister Rhoda. Up from the country for a couple of days' shopping. A nice pensive woman, older than her brother, looking like an engraving of George Eliot, heavy dark hair peacefully parted in the middle, Victorian brooch, a long romantic poem. A woman you see talking to gardeners, walking on lawns, driving off in a little car to local education committees. A botanist too, in a religious way. We talked about a bowl of white peonies in the drawing room. 'Paeonia,' she said. She was very reserved and shy. She said the plant had been introduced into Cornwall by the Brethren of Saint Michael. In the thirteenth century. She wouldn't interest you, Karvo, she's a good woman."

"She doesn't," said Karvo.

"Quite a medieval evening up till then," said Chatty. "Suddenly Ronnie, the husband, says, 'Pussy, you must *show* them!' As he says this he gives a lick of glee to his lips and his hands jump about in his trouser pockets. 'Oh, Doggie,' she says. 'Shall I be naughty? It's dreadful, dearest Chatty. Hats, Chatty! I've robbed the Place Vendôme. Bring your champagne.' "

And Chatty told how her weak thin hand took his—he

could feel all the bones in it—attached to an arm of steel. He was nearly dead, he said, by the time they all got up the long curving staircase, not from the climb so much as from sinking almost to the ankles in the hush of a deep yellow stair carpet. The four of them arrived in a large bedroom that had three high wide windows, the bay swelling over the lawn of the Crescent. But Chatty imagined from what was going on on the walls of the room that he was in the Burmese jungle. He wouldn't have been surprised, he said, to see the violet bottoms of mandrills sitting in the branches. Furry animals, like animal royalty, were spread on the floor. There was a golden bed, a Cleopatra's barge. Ronnie's sister stood apart. She had obviously seen it all before, and as beauties often do, looked unwell. Ronnie's face had stopped nodding. His mouth opened and he looked like a man congratulating himself on being about to be turned into a tiger, for Christine took a little run, almost a flight, to a wardrobe—"

"Don't bother about the wardrobe," said Karvo.

"—she pulled the doors open and out fell an enormous heap of hats, like a cloud of petals on the floor. About eighty of them. I spilled my champagne down my tie," said Chatty. "It was the least I could do. Let me go on. 'She'll wear them all,' Ronnie says. 'Pussy, is your back tired? She has to rest her back.' 'Doggie,' she says and pouts. Rhoda, the sister, is still standing apart. She is not drinking. She is a healthy woman who likes country walks, but when the hats come tumbling out she swells up and goes red in the face as if she is struggling against a pain in the chest. The stairs, of course. Heart, I suppose—all those stairs."

So, Chatty said, he tried to calm her by asking where she lived in the country, and she said she lived this side of Bath and he told her his aunt had a farm on the far side of the city and how he went down there for weekends. "It's your part of the country too," he said to Christine. "How nice, how strange.

"Always be careful when you talk to girls, Karvo," said Chatty. "Profit by my experience. She said I was mixing her up with Ann. Ann came from Bath. *She* came from Yorkshire."

"What of it?" said Karvo.

"Didn't your first girl friend ever slice you in half with a look?" said Chatty.

Karvo had stopped listening, so Chatty got down to business.

"We went downstairs to the Albigenses."

Ronnie edged him into a wall against a small Soutine as if about to give him extremely private information about a foreign government.

" 'The return to the twelfth century,' Ronnie says, 'it's absolutely *the* modern subject. It's the world today. Religious wars, mass murder, the crushing of small cultures. The Inquisition. It went on for a century. They appealed to the Pope, of course.' 'Dear dreadful Pope Innocent,' Christine called across. 'The Stalin of the time,' says Ronnie bearing down closer. 'Tortures. The Provençal nobility appear in crowds on the scene.' "

Chatty gathered there was a sort of liberal called the Duc d'Aquitaine trying to keep the peace, but the murder of Peter of Castelnau brought Pope Innocent's storm troops down from the north.

"Castelnau, weren't they cousins?" says Christine to her husband. And to Chatty: "The Johnsons came originally from Toulouse."

The sister interrupts. "Putney," she says.

"You'll find it in the Cistercian records," says Christine. "Or you can look it up in Schmidt or in Vaissete."

It was a piquant moment, Chatty said. There you had on the one hand a scholarly genealogist who could slip back to the thirteenth century as easy as pie but who, to be frank, was a *belle laide*, especially when she showed her teeth, being challenged by a peaceful botanist who had a corner in monkish gardening.

"I enjoyed it," said Chatty to Karvo. "It took me back to the old days in Paris. I'm afraid the two ladies don't get on."

Karvo put on his martyred look.

"It was all right," said Chatty. "Ronnie saved the situation. A born diplomat. He started telling me about the children of light and the children of darkness and finished up talking about the Perfecti."

Karvo looked up.

"It's not a cigar," said Chatty.

The Johnsons asked Karvo to dinner.

"That woman's electric. You're wrong about her book," said Karvo to Chatty when he came back. "I read the passages you marked. Wow! There's a story. She's going places."

When the mid-Atlantic slick flooded into Karvo's English, Chatty knew that one of what he called Karvo's Seasons was about to begin.

"I think," said Karvo, "you offended her. Did you say something?"

"Something rude about the thirteenth century, I expect," said Chatty.

"No, something's bugging her," said Karvo.

"I left with Rhoda that evening. We walked down the side of the park under the trees," said Chatty. "Perhaps it was that. Now Rhoda, there's a woman. She knows the names of flowers. Too plump for you, Karvo. And forty. She's the complete English lady. So beautifully conventional and uncandid, quiet but deep, you know—when they talk about their neighbors you aren't sure whether they are people or rhododendrons; whether the Winstanleys, say, are a breed of cattle or the county education committee or an asparagus bed. A good green-fingered woman—knows what is ranunculaceous and what is not. In human life, I mean. The only trouble is that they are always doing something for others. Lovely summer night and all she can do is to ask me the name of Christine's professor in Paris. One of her neighbors wants to send her daughter there."

"What are you talking about?" said Karvo.

"I'm talking about love," said Chatty. "Not as you know it. I could love a woman like that."

"I want a treatment for this story," said Karvo. And with that, Karvo's Albigensian period began. The word "massacre" had caught him. So had "torture." So had "incest." So had Christine. His head filled up with crime, sex and churches, Romanesque towers, medieval obscenities, antiques. After a month he bought a Van Gogh —and wouldn't say what he gave for it—one of the painter's swirling cornfields, done in the asylum. It matched his mood. He galloped over the Pyrenees with the incestuous rebel couple. Everywhere he went—to expensive restaurants, embassies and house parties—Christine and her husband were there. They gave enormous parties.

"They never ask me," said Chatty.

"You know, of course," Karvo said, "she's a Castelnau. That's why she wrote the book."

"No," said Chatty. "That's her husband."

"I don't take to him," said Karvo. "You've got it wrong."

"I think," said Chatty, "they're both Castelnaus. There's a Castelnau Road in Putney."

"That's not surprising," said Karvo, briefly a historian. "The survivors and descendants of the Albigenses split up, half joined up with the Huguenots and went to Bordeaux and the other half to England. They made a fortune in cotton. That's where she gets her money. She told me her brother's still got the place in Toulouse."

"Incidentally, the Castelnaus were on the wrong side —in the pay of the Pope. Did she mention it?" said Chatty. "Of course, I know one should never trust one's ancestors. Does Dolly get on with her?" Chatty asked, speaking of Karvo's latest wife.

"You know what women are about clothes. I'm taking Dolly to Paris," said Karvo.

"My aunt is not well. I'm off to the country," Chatty said.

There were long seasons in Karvo's life; there were short ones when he was between pictures. Seasons were apt to turn into cycles. The summer passed. The winds of early September were bashing the country gardens. "The hollyhocks are flat on their backs," Rhoda wrote in a note to Chatty. She added a postscript saying, "I discovered the professor's name—it was Ducros." Grit was blowing into Chatty's office window as he read the treatment.

"The story has no shape or end," he said to Karvo. "What does it mean, what is the message?"

Karvo spread his arms wide and held them in the air. Seeing nothing in them he began to reach for a button on his desk.

"I'll tell you what it means, what we have got to bring out," Chatty said. He stood up and recited, "The massacre of the Albigensians meant the final disappearance of the great medieval culture of Provence. It was lost forever to European civilization."

Karvo was suspicious, then appalled. He changed physically before Chatty's eyes. The word "culture" piled up like a wall that got larger every day. He stared at all that masonry and boredom settled on him.

"Funny," he said, "those are the very words Christine used."

"They're in the script," said Chatty.

"It is true," he went on, looking at a pill on the palm of his hand and then swallowing it, "nothing lasts."

The learned Christine had cooked her goose, so Chatty said, with a phrase. In the following weeks she and the Albigensian heresy were done for.

"Write her a note," said Karvo. "There's a good fellow."

"No," said Chatty. "She's your baby. She dropped me. I burn with resentment. I still can't think what I did."

"It's personally embarrassing," said Karvo, lifting his blotter and pretending to look for something.

"Much more for me—old time's sake, you know," said Chatty. "Get Phillips to do it." Phillips managed Karvo's company. "Dear Mrs. Johnson, we have now had a full breakdown of the costs, etc., etc. . . . He is a master of the commercial lament."

The letter was sent and Chatty returned the manuscript.

"My office seems empty without it—modern almost," said Chatty. "Sad. You meet your childhood sweetheart again and then—nothing."

He waited for the inevitable aftermath of Karvo's dreams: he would hear Christine's syllables freezing the man who ignorantly rejected Provençal culture and the birthplace of the Castelnaus.

But there was no reply. After a few weeks the manuscript was returned by the post office.

"Unknown" was written across it in pencil by an enthusiastic hand.

Chatty telephoned to the house. No manservant answered. He heard the voice of the cook. She had come in, she said, to collect her things before the removal men got them. You could trust no one today. The Johnsons had gone to their house in Paris and Mrs. Johnson had gone to Toulouse—her brother had died—such difficulties about the estate! The cook did not know the address. The London house had been sold. She was damping the telephone wires with her tears.

"Such troubles," she said.

An inexplicable hole had opened in London social life. It was as if whole streets, indeed the Crescent itself, had been removed, as if the map had been changed, without consultation, overnight, and nonentity had supervened.

"Anyone could see there was trouble there," Karvo said. "Ronnie Johnson was an adventurer. He came in, stripped her of every cent she had. I heard him talking to a Greek banker at the Hollinsheds about the trouble she was having about getting money out of France."

"I'll find out where she is from Rhoda," said Chatty.

"Forget it," said Karvo.

"I don't want to talk about it on the telephone. May I come and see you?" Chatty heard Rhoda's clear harvesting voice gathering sheaves of moral beauty as it came across the hills, the fields and the woods, the gardens and the village churches from the borders of Somerset. Partridge shooting had begun.

When Chatty was clearing up after Karvo's passages through people's lives he usually took the grander casualties to The Hundred and Five, but it was closed for redecoration, and Chatty was obliged to ask Rhoda to The Spangle. This little club was hardly the place for a lady from the country and one who could never be a casualty. The Spangle would be packed with people whose checks bounced and whom "one had never met." By nine in the evening, couples were hunched and whispering nose to nose across the gingham cloth of their tables, listening not to each other but for erotic news from the table behind them. It was a place for other people's confessions. There was the hope of being refreshed by scenes breaking out now and then. Les, the proprietor, who wore a cowboyish shirt, was a big-bellied, soft man with heavy spongy arms, white as suet pudding. He was in his sixties and was damp and swollen with the public secrets of his customers. Most people came in asking for someone else.

"Was John in last night?"

Les would perhaps reply, "Sarah was asking for him," or "I had a card from Flo. She's in Spain," or "Phil can't leave his dog," or, flatly, "Ada's barred."

Rhoda was wearing a cardigan, a green blouse, a tweed skirt and good walking shoes, but Chatty saw her face had changed. The sad George Eliot gaze had gone. The thick smooth black hair had been cropped into a variety of lengths so that she looked as if she had been pulled, not unwillingly, through a hedge—that is to say, younger. Victory, even giddiness, was in her beautiful brown eyes. Les stared with suspicion and offense at any new woman guest brought into the club and scarcely nodded to her when Chatty introduced her, but Rhoda did not mind. She sat down, and, after an efficient look around her, said, "What a killing place." The word "killing" made Chatty happy; it was so lyrically out of date.

"Tell me who everyone is," she said.

"Les is in a bit of a mood tonight," Chatty began by apologizing for Les. "He's on the watch for people who forgot to bring him a present for his birthday. He used to be an actor."

So Chatty and Rhoda fell to whispering and looking around like everyone else. He thought he was in for a restful evening and started talking about his farm. He looked at her and saw starlings flocking, avenues of elms. Rhoda allowed this, then abruptly she said, "So you turned down Christine's film?"

Chatty's face twitched. Experienced in consoling discarded actresses and mistresses, he had little experience in consoling authors. He certainly did not know how to begin with an author's relatives.

"The sad fact is," he said, "that the best films are made out of bad books, not out of good ones."

He saw the formidable Rhoda appear.

"That is not true," she said with the quiet authority of a thoughtful life. He now saw himself in for an ethical evening. But he was wrong again. She was too firm or too gentle to argue. He ordered their meal and he saw her pursuing truth placidly on her own through a large plateful of whitebait, a fish that would have given him gout within an hour.

"It is always embarrassing turning down the work of a friend," he said. "One always does it at the wrong moment. Family crisis, brother dying—actually dead, I believe. I hear Christine's in Toulouse. For the funeral, I suppose."

Rhoda, a frugal woman, scrupulously ate the last small fish and then drank a glass of white wine straight off. He noted the care of the first operation, the abandon of the second.

"That is what I want to talk to you about," she said.

Les was calling to a young woman: "Hullo, darling. Where's Stephen? Andrew was asking for him."

"Stephen," whispered Chatty, "has forgotten Leslie's birthday."

But Rhoda had lost interest in the killing aspect of the club.

"They are not in Toulouse," she said.

"Perhaps it was Paris, I forget," said Chatty.

"Christine's brother is not dead. She hasn't got a brother."

"But surely!" Chatty said. If there was one thing he remembered about the Christine of so many years ago, it was Christine telling him of her brother, retired from the Navy, living in the South of France, growing his own wine—"the head of the family," with its old-fashioned overtones of solid money, family councils, trusts, wills, marriages, crests on the silver and so on, and the weary care of her voice as she threw away her brother's distinctions; the phrase had stuck with him. He had read it in novels. To hear it spoken had been one of those instances of a forgotten piece of social history flying out of the past into the present like a stone coming through a window.

"Paul, the head of the family," said Chatty.

Seeing Rhoda's eyes studying him, he lost his confidence.

"Perhaps it was Ann's brother. One of them had a brother. It's a long time ago," he said.

"I've never met Ann," said Rhoda. "But I am quite certain Christine hasn't got a brother."

Chatty backed out, for he saw the truth seeker in Rhoda's eyes.

"Or I may be mixing it up with the book," he said. "The girl who went off with her brother."

"I haven't read the book," said Rhoda with a flick of the whip in her voice.

Chatty started telling the story, but she interrupted.

"There is *no* family," she said.

"But she comes from the north," Chatty said. "Yorkshire or somewhere. She said so at dinner. Her mother died, the father was killed in an air raid. There was just this brother."

"Her mother died," said Rhoda, "but her father and her stepmother are still alive. Not in the north of England. They've never been near it. They live less than twenty miles from you, the other side of Bath. They run a small public house."

Chatty saw that pile of pink, white and lacy hats come tumbling out of her wardrobe like butterflies and heard Christine's voice saying, "No, I am a Yorkshire woman. You're thinking of Ann."

"I have been to see them," said Rhoda. "They haven't seen or heard of Christine for sixteen years. Her father used to be a seed salesman. They haven't heard a thing about her since she was a student in Paris. They didn't even know she was married. Their name is Till. She has a sister who runs the place, a nice girl, but it's an awful pub. The father retired there to drink the profits. He said, 'Tell that girl if she comes near here I'll get my belt out.' "

The waitress brought boeuf bourgignon for Rhoda and, for Chatty, a sole. What an appetite she had! Rhoda continued at once her pursuit of the truth in silence through the food. Chatty gaped at his fish.

"This is good," she said at last. "You're letting yours get cold. I found them through the headmistress of her school. I am on the Education Committee. She said Christine was the cleverest girl they had ever had."

It was a principle of Chatty's to believe everything he was told, but now the very fish on his plate seemed opposed to him. It had been served on the bone and he hesitated to put his knife to it for fear of what he would find inside. He moved his mind to Paris. He saw a heavy black sweater, a pair of twisted stockings, a student's notebook on a café table.

"I can't believe it," said Chatty. "Hundreds of girls leave home, I know . . . They turn up in this place . . ."

"The London house is sold, the bailiffs have the pictures. Ronnie is at home with us. He has left her—thank God."

"Oh dear," said Chatty.

"The film," said Rhoda, "was her last throw. In the last ten years she has run through more than a hundred thousand pounds of Ronnie's money," said Rhoda. "One hundred thousand."

Rhoda changed before Chatty's eyes. The twined leafy branches that had seemed to frame the pensive face of the rural botanist dissolved. He saw instead the representative of a huge family trust.

"Where is she now?" he said.

"In a nursing home," she snapped at him. "I know where I'd put her!"

Chatty put down his knife and fork. He could not bear the sad color of the fish.

"Poor Christine," he said, looking at it.

"Poor Christine!" said Rhoda loudly, indeed addressing the club. The quiet oval face became square and the country skin flushed to a dark red. "Poor Ronnie, you mean. She has ruined him."

"They were rather going it, of course," said Chatty. "I suppose Ronnie knew what he was doing. What does he say?"

"He knew nothing until ten days ago. Nothing at all about her. Lies from the beginning to the end."

And when she said "Lies," Rhoda shouted.

The customers of The Spangle looked up and glanced at one another with joy. A row! That shout was in the genuine tradition of the club. Everyone was at home. At such moments the quarreling parties usually called for more drink. Les stepped behind the bar ready to get it. Rhoda corrected herself.

"Lies," she said quietly. "Pure invention."

"Ronnie *must* have known," Chatty said. "How did he find out?"

"He didn't. I did. Ronnie knew nothing, absolutely nothing. I had had my suspicions when he brought her down to stay before they were married; I couldn't stand her delivery."

Chatty raised the bottle to Rhoda's glass and he filled his own.

"It took time," said Rhoda. "You've known her longer than any of us," she said, "did she ever say or do . . ."

She stopped. She saw Chatty's face, so rakishly marked by the lines of his illnesses, smooth out and another face set very hard upon it. She was going to accuse him next. The pursuit of truth was going too far. Rhoda's voice had lost its note of moral beauty. He was thinking of the postscript to her note: "The name of the professor is Ducros." She had been hunting then.

"Mr. Chatterton," she said. "I love my brother. He is everything to me. He always will be. We have always been close all our lives since we were children. He is something very rare—a good man. I would die for him. I knew I was right about that girl. He is easily deceived. It isn't the money. I hate what she has done to him. I love my brother more than anything in the world."

How many times Chatty had heard the word "love" spoken at The Spangle by girls with globes of tears hanging in their eyes, by girls with their teeth set, by girls with their mouths twisted by rage. He patted their hands, told their fortunes, made up love affairs of his own—generally the most successful way of soothing them. He had the sad story of the girl who was in a Swiss sanatorium with him; they had both lost a lung. Such affectionate creatures all these girls were! They forgot their rages when they heard this, and looking at him with contented superstition, as if he were a talisman, their eyes cleared, glanced around the room and began their eternal quest once more.

But Rhoda was not in their case. She gazed at him not asking for help, but with the self-possession of one born for a single passion. In twenty years' time that look would be unalterably there. She not only loved, she was avenged. She had not given up until she had got her brother back. Chatty wished that victory in love would look more becoming.

"It is extraordinary, I agree, and I am sure if you say so, it is true," said Chatty.

"Every word," said Chatty.

"And a hundred thousand pounds is a lot of money."

"It's not only the money," she said.

"Well, I don't see really, if you think about it, what harm has been done. Ronnie was having the time of his life. He obviously adored her—"

"He was tricked."

"—buying her houses, taking her round, enjoying a splash, showering her with Renoirs and hats. With a

brain like hers she might still be sitting on the steps of
the British Museum eating a sandwich out of a paper bag.
He must have liked it. Quite frankly, she isn't a beauty.
Ronnie created her."

"She deceived him."

"I think he knew," said Chatty. "I expect he'd been
bored up to then. Boredom makes you close your eyes
and take the plunge."

"She's such a snob. That accent!" said Rhoda.

"Pedantic," he said. "Scholars often are. Anyway, one
gets used to accents in the theater."

He saw he was annoying her.

"It's really a fairy tale, isn't it?" he said. "Ronnie
waved a wand."

For a moment he thought she was going to lean across
the table and hit him. He sat back and recited:

> " 'The Owl and the Pussy-Cat went to sea
> In a beautiful sea-green boat.
> They took some honey, and plenty of money,
> Wrapped up in a five-pound note.' "

The poem was too much for her. A tear dropped down
her cheek.

"You've got the line wrong," she said, struggling
against the pain. "It was a *pea*-green boat.

"It was all those scholarships that gave her away. I
traced them back," she said bitterly.

The situation became too clear for Chatty. He did not
wish to see, too distinctly, the good woman who in a
passion of jealousy had hunted her sister-in-law down.
He was disturbed by a wish that Christine and not Rhoda
were sitting before him. He gave a number of dry
coughs, but he could not cough the wish away.

"Diana," Chatty called the waitress, an overworked
girl who had the habit of keeping a cigarette burning on

a saucer by the kitchen hatch, "if you'll bring me a packet
of cigarettes I'll marry you."

"You, Mr. Chatterton!" said the girl. "That'll be the
day."

"It's desperate."

The girl saw Rhoda's tears and pulled a face. The
Spangle liked tears. She fetched the cigarettes. Chatty
stood the packet on end considering it, not with passion
but with lust. Rhoda saw the packet through her tears.

"You can't! You mustn't," she said strictly. Chatty
picked up the packet and held it to his nose.

"Lovely temptation," he said, touching the packet with
his lips and putting it down again. Rhoda's tears had
stopped. In none of Chatty's experiences at The Spangle
had he ever known that a packet of cigarettes could bring
tears to a sudden end.

"Did they have any children?" Chatty asked.

"No—that is one blessing."

"Perhaps that was the trouble?" said Chatty.

The expression on the good woman's face was one of
horror so deep that she was silent.

And now Les came to their table, ignoring Rhoda.

"How's Karvo?" he asked. "Maggy was asking for
him."

"Oh God!" said Chatty.

"Who is Maggy?" asked Rhoda when Les walked off.

"It's a long story. Too personal. Some other time. I'm
thinking about Christine. What a performance—one has
to admit."

"I don't think that remark is appropriate," said Rhoda.
"There's a time when sympathy stops. I think of her
sometimes. What a hell she must have lived in knowing
every day for years that she might be found out."

The satisfaction in Rhoda's voice shocked Chatty. He
gave up trying to charm her.

"Oh, I don't think conscience troubled her at all," he

said gaily. "I don't think she was in hell. That is what I mean by performance. She knew her part in every detail. It must have thrilled her to act it, adding a little touch every day. Only an academic could do that! Its a pretty commonplace everyday story really, but to her—what a triumph! What documentation! Imagine her memory! And making Ronnie love it."

"Not now," said Rhoda. "She has lost him for good."

"That is true," said Chatty. "The really sad thing is that she has lost Paul."

"You are infuriating," said Rhoda. "He *never existed,* I tell you."

"I know. She invented him. That is what makes it worse. She has lost her only real friend."

Chatty was glad to see that the perfect Rhoda looked troubled.

"What you are saying is that I did wrong," she said.

"I think you did what you *wanted* to do," said Chatty.

"I can see," she said, "that you don't like me. Hasn't anyone any moral sense nowadays? You knew her. I thought it was my duty to tell you. That was my only motive."

Rhoda picked up her handbag.

"Diana, my sweetheart," Chatty called to the waitress. "I seem to want my bill."

They sat silently until the bill came and then Rhoda said, "Thank you for a lovely evening. You must drive over and see us sometime. Ronnie would like that."

Karvo said to Chatty, "A hundred thousand pounds? Who told you?"

"Clothilde," said Chatty. "She was on the Pope's side. You remember the Albigensians . . ."

"We didn't make it," said Karvo.

"I know," said Chatty. "I mean the escape of the lovers over the Pyrenees, but Clothilde is with them. She has tracked down the incest story and she betrays them to the Inquisition out of jealousy. Rhoda Johnson. Another tragedy in my life. I've seen into the heart of a good woman. Never do that."

Karvo ignored this.

"It was a Swedish story really," said Karvo furtively. "The Swedes could do it."

"No, not Swedish, not even Albigensian—very English, west country. The brother's name was Paul, purely imaginary. Still, his estate was useful naturally as capital security, especially when he died."

"Who are we talking about?" said Karvo.

"Christine's brother, Paul," said Chatty.

"But he's dead."

"You don't listen," Chatty said. "Think of what he was going to leave her. Did she ever mention it to you?"

"Yes," said Karvo, surprised. "She did. Why?"

"Historians go mad. All that research and detail work gets them down. They crack up. Get delusions of grandeur, and in two minutes, they are popping in their personal story. They're badly paid, too. She needed the money. You can't blame them," said Chatty.

"When did the Johnsons leave?" said Karvo.

"They didn't leave. She's had a breakdown. She is in a nursing home."

"Yes, you told me—when was that?"

"Weeks and weeks ago." Chatty took out his diary. "October fourth."

Then Chatty saw Karvo do an extraordinary thing. The man who couldn't remember his wife's birthday, the martyr who was always in trouble because he could not remember the dates of his several wedding anniversaries, the man for whom everything was done by secretaries, the man who was entirely public, surprised Chatty by the secretive way in which he now performed a private action. He took out a pocket diary. Chatty had seen

Karvo do this only once before when he was ill; indeed Karvo had shown him a page with an X and a figure written against it. The first Tuesday in every month he recorded his weight. He opened the diary now and said, "October fourth—that's what *I've* got. Why did you make a note of it?"

"A sense of loss," said Chatty. "She'd gone."

"I didn't know she meant anything to you," said Karvo bashfully.

"There it is," said Chatty. "Nor did I. One thinks of it at night."

"Chatty . . ." Karvo began. "Well, no—I don't want to pry into your private affairs."

"Oh no, there was nothing like that in it. I liked her best when she was dirty and fat. I asked them both down to the farm but she wouldn't come. It rather hurt at the time, but I see it now. It might have saved them, even both of them."

Karvo pressed the button and asked for his chauffeur to be sent round.

"A hundred thousand pounds," said Karvo, but in the fond, impersonal, admiring manner of one who sees yet one more piece of financial history pass down the Thames, under the bridges and out to sea.

"Tell the chauffeur to wait," said Chatty. "Karvo, I don't want to pry into *your* private affairs. I want to ask you about ours—yours and mine."

Karvo saw no escape from Chatty when the lines of his face smoothed out.

"All right, if that is what you want to know, she's as frigid as stone," said Karvo. "I tried—well, not actually tried—at the Hollinsheds'."

"Oh I know *that*," said Chatty. "I discovered that in Paris years ago. I was just finding out when Ronnie Johnson knocked at my door. A very innocent fellow—he didn't realize what was going on. Or perhaps he did. I remember he nodded. Don't let's talk about it. What I want to know is how much she touched you for on October fourth? She got fifty pounds out of me. I made a note of it."

"You fool," boasted Karvo. "She got seven hundred and fifty out of me, guaranteed by the estate."

"Paul's," said Chatty.

Karvo had a special way of falling into speechlessness. He would lean back in his chair, then would seem to be making a quick inventory of everything in the office, then close his eyes. It was as if he was under an anesthetic at the dentist's. His inner life would become brilliant with ridiculous dramas, and when he came round, panting, he would see what he must do. He came round now.

"I can get it off expenses," he said. "Why did you do it, Chatty?"

"Oh, you know—the pathos of the rich."

Karvo grunted and got up.

"Can I drop you anywhere?"

"No," said Chatty. "I'm going to try and see Christine."

"Don't be a fool," said Karvo. "You'll never get it back."

"That is not what I'm going for," said Chatty. "She's alone."

The Spree

THE old man—but when does old age begin?—the old man turned over in bed and putting out his hand to the crest of his wife's beautiful white rising hip and comforting bottom, hit the wall with his knuckles and woke up. More than once during the two years since she had died he had done this and knew that if old age vanished in the morning it came on at night, filling the bedroom with people until, switching on the light, he saw it staring at him; then it shuffled off and left him looking at the face of the clock. Three hours until breakfast: the hunger of loss yawned under his ribs. Trying to make out the figures on the clock he dropped off to sleep again and was walking up Regent Street seeing, on the other side of it, a very high bred white dog, long in the legs and distinguished in its step, hurrying up to Oxford Circus, pausing at each street corner in doubt, looking up at each person as he passed and whimpering politely to them: "Me? Me? Me?" and going on when they did not answer. A valuable dog like that, lost! Someone will pick it up, lead it off, sell it to the hospital and doctors will cut it up! The old man woke up with a shout to stop the crime and then he saw daylight in the room and heard bare feet running past his room and the shouts of his three grandchildren and his daughter-in-law calling "Ssh! Don't wake Grandpa."

The old man got out of bed and stood looking indignantly at the mirror over the washbasin and at his empty gums. It was awful to think, as he put his teeth in to cover the horror of his mouth, that twelve or fourteen hours of London daylight were stacked up meaninglessly waiting for him. He pulled himself together. As he washed, listening to the noises of the house, he made up a speech to say to his son who must be downstairs by now.

"I am not saying I am ungrateful. But old and young are not meant to be together. You've got your life. I've got mine. The children are sweet—you're too sharp with them—but I can't stand the noise. I don't want to live at your expense. I want a place of my own. Where I can breathe. Like Frenchy." And as he said this, speaking into the towel and listening to the tap running, he could see and hear Frenchy, who was his dentist but who looked like a rascally prophet in his white coat and was seventy if he was a day, saying to him as he looked down into his mouth and as if he was really tinkering with a property there, "You ought to do what I've done. Get a house by the sea. It keeps you young."

Frenchy vanished, leaving him ten years younger. The old man got into his shirt and trousers and was carefully spreading and puffing up his sparse black and gray hair across his head when in came his daughter-in-law, accusing him—why did she accuse? "Grandpa! You're up!"

She was like a soft Jersey cow with eyes too big and reproachful. She was bringing him tea, the dear sweet tiresome woman.

"Of course I'm up," he said.

One glance at the tea showed him it was not like the tea he used to make for his wife when she was alive, but had too much milk in it, always tepid, left standing somewhere. He held his hairbrush up and he suddenly said, asserting his right to live, to get out of the house, in air he could breathe, "I'm going in to London to get my hair cut."

"Are you sure you'll be all right?"

"Why do you say that?" he said severely. "I've got several things I want to do."

And when she had gone, he heard her say on the stairs, "He's going to get his hair cut!"

And his son saying, "Not again!"

This business, this defiance of the haircut! For the old man it was not a mere scissoring and clipping of the hair. It was a ceremonial of freedom; it had the whiff of orgy, the incitement of a ritual. As the years went by leaving him in such a financial mess that he was now down to not much more than a pension, it signified desire—but what desire? To be memorable in some streets of London, or at least, as evocative as an incense. The desire would come to him, on summer days like this, when he walked in his son's suburban garden, to sniff and to pick a rose for his buttonhole; and then, already intoxicated, he marched out of the garden gate onto the street and to the bus stop, upright and vigorous, carrying his weight well and pink in the face. The scents of the barber's had been creeping into his nostrils, his chest, even went down to his legs. To be clipped, oiled and perfumed was to be free.

So on this decent July morning in the sun-shot and acid suburban mist, he stood in a queue for the bus, and if anyone had spoken to him he would have gladly said, to put them in their place, "Times have changed. Before I retired, when Kate was alive—though I must honestly say we often had words about it—I always took a cab."

The bus came and whooshed him down to Knightsbridge, to his temple—the most expensive of the big shops. There, reborn on miles of carpet he paused and sauntered, sauntered and paused. He was inflamed by hall after hall of women's dresses and hats, by cosmetics and jewelry. Scores of women were there. Glad to be cooled off, he passed into the echoing hall of provisions.

He saw the game, the salmon and the cheese. He ate them and moved on to lose twenty years in the men's clothing department, where, among ties and brilliant shirts and jackets, his stern yet bashful pink face woke up to the loot and his ears heard the voices of the rich, the grave chorus of male self-approval. He went to the end where the oak stairs led down to the barber's; there, cool as clergy, they stood gossiping in their white coats. One came forward, seated him and dressed him up like a baby. And then—nothing happened. He was the only customer, and the barber took a few steps back toward the group saying, "He wasn't at the staff meeting."

The old man tapped his finger irritably under his sheet. Barbers did not cut hair, it seemed. They went to staff meetings. One called back, "Mr. Holderness seconded it."

Who was Holderness?

"Where is Charles?" said the old man to call the barbers to order. Obsequiously, the man began that pretty music with his scissors.

"Charles?" said the barber.

"Yes. Charles. He shaved me for twenty years."

"He retired."

Another emptiness, another cavern, opened inside the old man.

"Retired? He was a child!"

"All the old ones have retired."

The barber had lost his priestly look. He looked sinful, even criminal, certainly hypocritical.

And although the old man's head was being washed by lotions and oils and there was a tickling freshness about the ears and his nostrils quickened, there was something uneasy about the experience. In days gone by, the place had been baronial, now it seemed not quite to gleam. One could not be a sultan among a miserable remnant of men who held staff meetings. When the old man left, the woman at the desk went on talking as she took his money and did not know his name. When he went upstairs, he paused to look back—no, the place was a palace of pleasure no longer. It was the place where—except for the staff—no one was known.

And that was what struck him as he stepped out of the glancing swing doors of the shop, glad to be out in the July sun: that he was a sultan, cool, scented and light-headed, extraordinary in a way, sacred almost, ready for anything—but cut off from expectancy, unknown nowadays to anybody, free for nothing, liberty evaporating out of the tips of his shoes. He stepped out on the pavement dissembling leisure. His walk became slower and gliding. For an hour, shop windows distracted him; new shops where old had been shocked him. But, he said, pulling himself together, I must not fall into *that* trap: old people live in the past. And I am not old! Old I am not! So he stopped gliding and stepped out willfully, looking so stern and with mouth turned down, so corrupt and purposeful with success, that he was unnoticeable. Who notices success?

It was always—he didn't like to admit it—like this on these days when he made the great stand for his haircut and the exquisite smell. He would set out with a vision, it crumbled into a rambling dream. He fell back, like a country hare, on his habitual run, to the shops which had bought his goods years ago, to see what they were selling and where he knew no one now; to a café which had changed its décor, where he ate a sandwich and drank a cup of coffee; but as the dream consoled, it dissolved into final melancholy. He with his appetite for everything, who could not pass a shop window, or an estate agent's, or a fine house, without greed watering in his mouth, could buy nothing. He hadn't the cash.

There was always this moment when the bottom began to fall out of his haircut days. He denied that his legs

were tired, but he did slow down. It would occur to him
suddenly in Piccadilly that he knew no one now in the
city. He had been a buyer and seller, not a man for
friends: he knew buildings, lifts, offices, but not people.
There would be nothing for it but to return home. He
would drag his way to the inevitable bus stop of defeat,
and stand, as so many Londoners did, with surrender on
their faces. He delayed it as long as he could, stopping
at a street corner or gazing at a passing girl and looking
around with that dishonest look a dog has when it is
pretending not to hear its master's whistle. There was
only one straw to clutch at. There was nothing wrong
with his teeth, but he could ring up his dentist. He could
ring up Frenchy. He could ring him and say, "Frenchy?
How's tricks?" Sportily and (a man for smells), he could
almost smell the starch in Frenchy's white coat, the keen,
chemical, hygienic smell of his room. The old gentleman
considered this and then went down a couple of disheart-
ened side streets. In a short cul-de-sac, standing outside
a urinal and a few doors from a dead-looking pub, there
was a telephone box. An oldish brown motor coach was
parked empty at the curb by it, its doors closed, a small
crowd waiting beside it. There was a man in the telephone box, but he came out in a temper, shouting something to the crowd. The old man went into the box. He
had thought of something to say, "Hullo, Frenchy!
Where is that house you were going to find me, you old
rascal?"

For Frenchy came up from the sea every day. It was
true that Frenchy was a rascal, especially with the
women, one after the other, but looking down into the
old man's mouth and chipping at a tooth he seemed to
be looking into your soul.

The old man got out his coins. He was tired but eagerness revived him as he dialed.

"Hullo, Frenchy," he said. But the voice that replied
was not Frenchy's. It was a child's. The child was calling

out, "Mum. Mum." The old man banged down the telephone and stared at the dial. His heart thumped. He had,
he realized, not dialed Frenchy's number but the number
of his old house, the one he had sold after Kate had died.

The old gentleman backed out of the box and
stared, tottering with horror, at it. His legs went weak,
his breath had gone and sweat bubbled on his face. He
steadied himself by the brick wall. He edged away from
the bus and the crowd so as not to be seen. He thought
he was going to faint. He moved to a doorway. There was
a loud laugh from the crowd as a young man with long
black hair gave the back of the bus a kick. And then,
suddenly, he and a few others rushed toward the old
man, shouting and laughing.

"Excuse us," someone said and pushed him aside. He
saw he was standing in the doorway of the pub.

"That's true," the old man murmured to himself.
"Brandy is what I need." And, at that, the rest of the little
crowd pushed into him or past him. One of them was a
young girl with fair hair who paused as her young man
pulled her by the hand and said kindly to the old man,
"After you."

There he was, being elbowed, traveling backward into
the little bar. It was the small private bar of the pub and
the old man found himself against the counter. The
young people were stretching their arms across him and
calling out orders for drinks and shouting. He was
wedged among them. The wild young man with the
piratical look was on one side of him, the girl and her
young man on the other. The wild young man called to
the others, "Wait a minute. What's yours, dad?"

The old man was bewildered. "Brandy."

"Brandy," shouted the young man across the bar.

"That's right," said the girl to the old man, studying
his face. "You have one. You ought to have got on the
first coach."

"You'd have been halfway to bloody Brighton by

now," said the wild young man. "The first bloody outing this firm's had in its whole bloody history and they bloody forgot the driver. Are you the driver?"

Someone called out, "No, he's not the driver."

"I had a shock," the old man began, but crowded against the bar no one heard him.

"Drink it up then," the girl said to him, and startled by her kindness, he drank. The brandy burned and in a minute fire went up into his head, and his face lost its hard bewildered look and it loosened into a smile. He heard their young voices flying about him. They were going to Brighton. No, the other side of Brighton. No, this side—well, to bloody Hampton's mansion, estate, something. The new chairman—he'd thrown the place open. Bloody thrown it, laughed the wild man, to the Works and the Office and, as usual, "the Works get the first coach." The young girl leaned down to smell the rose in the old man's buttonhole and said to her young man, "It's lovely. Smell it." His arm was round her waist and there were the two of them bowing to the rose.

"From your garden?" said the girl.

The old man heard himself, to his astonishment, tell a lie.

"I grew it," he said.

"We shan't bloody start for hours," someone said. "Drink up."

The old man looked at his watch: a tragic look. Soon they'd be gone. Someone said, "Which department are you in?" "He's in the Works," someone said. "No, I've retired," said the old man, not to cause a fuss. "Have another, dad," said the young man. "My turn."

Three of them bent their heads to hear him say again, "I have retired," and one of them said, "It was passed at the meeting. Anyone retired entitled to come."

"You've made a mistake," the old man began to explain to them. "I was just telephoning to my dentist . . ."

"No," said one of the bending young men, turning to someone in the crowd. "That bastard Fowkes talked a lot of bull but it passed."

"You're all right," the girl said to the old man.

"He's all right," said another and handed the old man another drink. If only they would stop shouting, the old man thought, I could explain.

"A mistake . . ." he began again.

"It won't do you any harm," someone said. "Drink up."

Then someone shouted from the door. "He's here. The driver."

The girl pulled the old man by the arm and he found himself being hustled to the door.

"My glass," he said.

He was pushed, holding his half-empty glass, into the street. They rushed past him and he stood there, glass in hand, trying to say Good-bye and then he followed them, still holding his glass, to explain. They shouted to him, "Come on," and he politely followed to the door of the bus where they were pushing to get in.

But at the door of the bus everything changed. A woman wearing a flowered dress with a red belt, a woman as stout as himself, had a foot on the step of the bus and was trying to heave herself up, while people ahead of her blocked the door. She nearly fell.

The old man, all smiles and sadness, put on a dignified anger. He pushed his way toward her. He turned forbiddingly on the youngsters.

"Allow me, madam," he said and took the woman's cool fat elbow and helped her up the step, putting his own foot on the lower one. Fatal. He was shoved up and himself pushed inside, the brandy spilling down his suit. He could not turn round. He was in, driven in deeply, to wait till the procession stopped. "I'm getting out," he said.

He flopped into the seat behind the woman.

"Young people are always in a rush," she turned to say
to him.

The last to get in were the young couple.

"Break it up," said the driver. They were slow, for they
were enlaced and wanted to squeeze in united.

The old man waited for them to be seated and then
stood up, glass in hand, as if offering a toast, as he moved
forward to get out.

"Would you mind sitting down," said the driver. He
was counting the passengers, and one, seeing the old
man with the glass in his hand, said, "Cheers."

For the first time in his adult life, the old man indignantly obeyed an order. He sat down, was about to explain his glass, heard himself counted, got up. He was
too late. The driver pulled a bar, slammed the door,
spread his arms over the wheel and off they went, to a
noise that bashed people's eyeballs.

At every change of the gears, as the coach gulped out
of the narrow streets, a change took place in the old man.
Shaken in the kidneys, he looked around in protest, put
his glass out of sight on the floor and blushed. He was
glad no one was sitting beside him, for his first idea was
to scramble to the window and jump through it at the
first traffic lights. The girl who had her arm round her
young man looked round and smiled. Then, he too
looked around at all these unknown people, belonging
to a firm he had never heard of, going to a destination
unknown to him, and he had the inflated sensations of
an enormous illegality. He had been kidnaped. He
tipped back his hat and looked bounderish. The bus was
hot and seemed to be frying in the packed traffic when
it stopped at the lights. People had to shout to be heard.
Under cover of the general shouting, he too shouted to
a couple of women across the gangway, "Do we pass the
Oval?"

The woman asked her friend, who asked the man in

front, who asked the young couple. Blocks of offices went by in lumps. No one knew except someone who said, "Must do." The old man nodded. The moment the Oval cricket ground came into sight, he planned to go to the driver and tell him to let him off. So he kept his eyes open, thinking, What a lark. What a thing to tell them at home. Guess what? Had a free ride. "Cheek, my boy" (he'd say to his son), "that's what you need. Let me give you a bit of advice. You'll get nowhere without cheek."

His pink face beamed with shrewd frivolity as the coach groaned over the Thames that had never looked so wide and sly. Distantly a power station swerved to the west, then to the east, then rocked like a cradle as the young girl—restless like Kate she was—got out of her young man's arms and got him back into hers, in a tighter embrace. Three containers passed, the coach slackened, then choked forward so suddenly that the old man's head nearly hit the back of the head of the fat lady in front. He studied it and noticed the way the woman's thick hair, gold with gray in it, was darker as it came out of her neck like a growing plant and he thought, as he had often done, how much better a woman's head looks from behind—the face interferes with it in front. And then his own chin went slack and he began a voluptuous journey down corridors. One more look at the power station, which had become several jumping power stations, giving higher and higher leaps in the air, and he was asleep.

A snore came from him. The talking woman across the gangway was annoyed by this soliloquizing noise which seemed to offer a rival narrative; but others admired it for its steadiness, which peacefully mocked the unsteady recovery and spitting and fading energy of the coach and the desperation of the driver. Between their shouts at the driver, many glanced admiringly at the sleeper. He was swinging in some private barber's shop that swerved through space, sometimes in some airy corridor, at other

times circling beneficently round a cricket match in
which Frenchy, the umpire, in his white linen coat, was
offering him a plate of cold salmon which his daughter-
in-law was trying to stop him from eating; he was off the
coach, striking his way home on foot at the tail of the
longest funeral procession he had ever seen, going uphill
for miles into fields that were getting greener and colder
and emptier as snow came on and he sat down plonk, out
of breath, waking to hear the weeping of the crowds, all
weeping for him, and then, still waking, he saw himself
outside the tall glass walls of a hospital. It must be a
hospital, for inside two men in white could be clearly
seen in a glass-enclosed room, one of them the driver,
getting ready to carry him in on a stretcher. He gasped,
now fully awake. There was absolute silence. The coach
had stopped; it was empty—he was alone in it, except for
the woman who, thank God, was still sitting in front of
him, the hair still growing from the back of her neck.

"Where . . ." he began. Then he saw the hospital was,
in fact, a garage. The passengers had got out, garagemen
were looking under the hood of the bus. The woman
turned round. He saw a mild face, without make-up.

"We've broken down," she said.

How grateful he was for her mild face. He had thought
he was dead.

"I've been asleep," he said. "Where are we?"

He nearly said, "Have we passed the Oval?" but swallowed that silly question.

"Quarter past three," he said. Meaning thirty miles
out, stuck fast in derelict country at a crossroads, with a
few villas sticking out in fields, eating into the grass
among a few trees, with a billboard on the far side of the
highway saying blatantly, MORTGAGES, and the cars dash-
ing by in flights like birds, twenty at a time, still weeping
away westward into space.

The woman had turned to study him, and when he got

up, flustered, she said in a strict but lofty voice, "Sit down."

He sat down.

"Don't you move," she said. "I'm not going to move. They've made a mess of it. Let them put it right."

She had twisted round and he saw her face, wide and full now, as meaty as an obstinate country girl's, and with a smile that made her look as though she were evaporating.

"This is Hampton's doing," she said. "Anything to save money. I am going to tell him what I think of him when I see him. No one in charge. Not even the driver —listen to him. Treat staff like cattle. They've got to send another coach. Don't you move until it comes."

Having said this, she was happy.

"When my husband was on the Board nothing like this happened. Do you know anyone here? *I* don't. Everything's changed."

She studied his gray hair.

The old man clung for the moment to the fact that he and she were united in not knowing anybody. His secretiveness was coming back.

"I've retired," he said.

The woman leaned further over the back of the seat and looked around the empty bus and then back at him as if she had captured him. Her full lips were the resting lips of a stout woman between meals.

"I must have seen you at the Works with John," she said. "It was always a family in those days. Or were you in the office?"

I must get out of this, the old man was thinking, and he sat forward nearer to her, getting ready to get out once more. I must find out the name of this place, get a train or a bus or something, get back home. The place looked nameless.

But since his wife had died he had never been as near

to a strange woman's face. It was a wide, ordinary, baby-like face damp in the skin, with big blue eyes under fair, skimpy eyebrows, and she studied him as a soft, plump child would—for no reason beyond an assumption that he and she were together in this: they weren't such fools, at their ages, to get off the coach. It was less the nearness of the face than her voice that kept him there.

It was a soft, high voice that seemed to blow away like a child's and was far too young for her, even sounded so purely truthful as to be false. It came out in deep breaths drawn up from soft but heavy breasts that could, he imagined, kick up a hullabaloo, a voice which suggested that by some silly inconsequent right she would say whatever came into her head. It was the kind of voice that made the old man swell with a polite, immensely intimate desire to knock the nonsense out of her.

"I can smell your rose from here," she said. "There are not many left who knew the firm in John's time. It was John's lifework."

He smiled complacently. He had his secret.

She paused and then the childish voice went suddenly higher. She was not simply addressing him. She was addressing a meeting.

"I told him that when he let Hampton flatter him he'd be out in a year. I said to John, 'He's jealous. He's been jealous all the time.'"

The woman paused. Then her chin and her lips stuck out, and her eyes that had looked so vague began to bulge and her voice went suddenly deep, rumbling with prophecy.

" 'He wants to kill you,' I said. You," said the woman to the old man, "must have seen it. And he did kill him. We went on a trip round the world: America, Japan, India"—her voice sailed across countries—"That's where he died. If Hampton thinks he can wipe it out by throwing his place open to the staff and getting me down there, on show, he's wrong."

My God, she's as dotty as Kate's sister used to get after her husband died, thought the old man. I'm sitting behind a madwoman.

"Dawson," she said and abruptly stood up as the old man rose too. "Oh," she said in her high regal style, gazing away out of the window of the bus. "I remember your name now. You had that row, that terrible row—oh yes," she said eagerly, the conspirator. "*You* ring up Hampton. He's afraid of you. He'll listen. I've got the number here. You tell him there are twenty-seven of his employees stranded on the Brighton road."

The old man sighed. He gave up all idea of slipping out. When a woman orders you about, what do you do? He thought she looked rather fine standing there prophetically. The one thing to do in such cases was to be memorable. When is a man most memorable? When he says "No."

"No, I wouldn't think of it," he said curtly. "Mr. Hampton and I are not on speaking terms."

"Why?" said the woman, distracted by curiosity.

"Mr. Hampton and I," he began, and he looked very gravely at her for a long time. "I have never heard of him. Who is he? I'm not on the staff. I've never heard of the firm." And then like a conjurer waving a handkerchief, he spread his face into a smile that had often got him an order in the old days.

"I just got on the coach for the ride. Someone said, 'Brighton.' 'Day at the sea,' I said. 'Suits me.' "

The woman's face went the color of liver with rage and disbelief. One for the law, all the rage she had just been feeling about Hampton now switched to the old man. She was unbelieving.

"No one checked?" she said, her voice throbbing. She was boiling up like the police.

The old gentleman just shook his head gently. "No one checked"—it was a definition of paradise. If he had wings he would have spread them, taken to the air and flown round her three times, saying, "Not a soul! Not a soul!"

She was looking him up and down. He stood with a plump man's dignity, but what saved him in her eyes were his smart, well-cut clothes, his trim hair and the jaunty rose: he looked like an old rip, a racing man, probably a crook—at any rate, a bit of a rogue on the spree, yet innocent too. She studied his shoes and he moved a foot and kicked the brandy glass. It rolled into the gangway and he smiled slightly.

"You've got a nerve," she said, her smile spreading.

"Sick of sitting at home," he said. Weighing her up— not so much her character but her body—he said, "I've been living with my daughter-in-law since my wife died."

He burst out with confidence, for he saw he had almost conquered her. "Young and old don't mix. Brighton would suit me. I thought I would have a look around for a house."

Her eyes were still busily going over him.

"You're a spark," she said, still staring. Then she saw the glass and bent down to pick it up. As she straightened she leaned on the back of the seat and laughed out loud.

"You just got on. Oh dear." She laughed loudly, help-lessly. "Serves Hampton right.

"Sit down," she said. He sat down. She sat down on the seat opposite. He was astonished and even shy to see his peculiar case appreciated, and his peculiarity grew in his mind from a joke to a poem, from a poem to a dogma.

"I meant to get off at the Oval, but I dropped off to sleep." He laughed.

"Going to see the cricket?" she said.

"No," he said. "Home—I mean my son's place."

The whole thing began to appear lovely to him. He felt as she laughed at him, as she still held the glass, twid-dling it by the stem, that he was remarkable.

"Years ago I did it once before," he said, multiplying

his marvels. "When my wife was alive. I got a late train
from London, went to sleep and woke up in Bath. I did.
I really did. Stayed at the Royal. Saw a customer next
day. He was so surprised to see me he gave me an order
worth three hundred pounds. My wife didn't believe
me."

"Well, can you blame her?" the woman said.

The driver walked from the office of the garage and
put his head into the coach and called out, "They're
sending a new bus. Be here four o'clock."

The old man turned. "By the way, I'm getting off," he
shouted to the driver.

"Aren't you going on?" said the woman. "I thought
you said you were having a trip to the sea."

She wanted him to stay.

"To be frank," said the old man. "These youngsters
—we'd been having a drink—they meant no harm—
pushed me on when I was giving you a hand. I was in the
pub. I had had a bit of a shock. I did something foolish.
Painful really."

"What was that?" she said.

"Well," said the old man swanking in his embarrass-
ment, and going very red. "I went to this telephone box,
you know, where the coach started from, to ring up my
dentist—Frenchy. I sometimes ring him up, but I got
through to the wrong number. You know what I did? I
rang the number of my old house, when Kate—when my
wife—was alive. Some girl answered—maybe a boy—I
don't know. It gave me a turn, doing a thing like that. I
thought my mind had gone."

"Well, the number would have changed."

"I thought, I really did think, for a second, it was my
wife."

The traffic on the main road sobbed or whistled as they
talked. Containers, private cars, police cars, breakdown
vans, cars with boats on their roofs—all sobbing their

hearts out in a panic to get somewhere else.

"When did your wife die?" said the woman. "Just recently?"

"Two years ago," he said.

"It was grief. That is what it was—grief," she said gravely and looked away from him into the sky outside and to the derelict bit of country.

That voice of hers, by turns childish, silly, passing to the higher notes of the exalted and belligerent widow— all that talk of partners killing each other!—had become, as his wife's used to do after some tantrum, simply plain.

Grief. Yes it was. He blinked away the threat of tears before her understanding. In these two years he seemed, because of his loneliness, to be dragging an increasing load of unsaid things behind him, things he had no one to tell. With his son and his daughter-in-law and their young friends he sat with his mouth open ready to speak, but he could never get a word out. The words simply fell back down his throat. He had a load of what people called boring things which he could not say: he had loved his wife; she had bored him; it had become a bond. What he needed was not friends, for since so many friends had died he had become a stranger; he needed another stranger. Perhaps like this woman whose face was as blank as his was, time having worn all expression from it. Because of that, you could see she looked now, if not as old as he was, full of life; but she had joined his lonely race and had lost the look of going nowhere. He lowered his eyes and became shy. Grief—what was it? A craving. Yet not for a face or even a voice or even for love, but for a body. But dressed. Say, in a flowered dress.

To get his mind off a thought so bold he uttered one of his boring things, a sort of sample of what he would have said to his wife. "Last night I had a dream about a dog," he began, to test her out as a stranger to whom you could say any damn silly thing. A friend would never listen to damn silly things.

The woman repeated, going back to what she had already said, as women do, "Remembering the telephone number—it was grief."

And then went off at a tangent, roughly. "Don't mention dreams to me. Last week at the bungalow I saw my husband walk across the sitting room clean through the electric fire and the mirror over the mantelpiece and stand on the other side of it, not looking at me, but saying something to me that I couldn't hear—asking for a box of matches, I expect."

"Imagination," said the old man, sternly correcting her. He had no desire to hear of her dead husband's antics, but he did feel that warm, already possessive desire, to knock sense into her. It was a pleasant feeling.

"It wasn't imagination," she said, squaring up to him. "I packed my things and went to London at once. I couldn't stand it. I drove in to Brighton, left the car at the station and came up to London for a few days. That is why when I heard about Hampton's party at the office I took this coach.

"Saved the train fare. Why shouldn't Hampton pay?" She grinned. "I told him I'd come to the party, but I'm not going. I'm picking up the car at Brighton and going home to the bungalow. It's only seven miles away."

She waited to see if he would laugh at their being so cunningly in the same boat. He did not laugh and that impressed her, but she frowned. Her husband would not have laughed either.

"I dread going back," she said sulkily.

"I sold my place," he said. "I know the feeling."

"You were right," said the woman. "That's what I ought to do. Sell the place. I'd get a good price for it, too. I'm not exactly looking forward to going back there this evening. It's very isolated—but the cat's there."

He said nothing. Earnestly she said, "You've got your son and daughter-in-law waiting for you," she said, giving him a pat on the knee. "Someone to talk to. You're lucky."

The driver put his head into the door and said, "All out. The other coach is here."

"That's us," said the woman.

The crowd outside were indeed getting into the new coach. The old man followed her out and looked back at the empty seats with regret. At the door he stepped past her and handed her out. She was stout but landed light as a feather. The wild young man and his friends were shouting, full of new beer, bottles in their pockets. The others trooped in.

"Good-bye," said the old man, doing his memorable turn.

"You're not coming with us?" said the woman. And then she said quietly, looking around secretively. "I won't say anything. You can't give up now. You're worried about your daughter-in-law. I know," she said.

The old man resented that.

"That doesn't worry me," he said.

"You ought to think of them," she said. "You ought to."

There was a shout of vulgar laughter from the wild young man and his friends. They had seen the two young lovers a long way off walking slowly, with all the time in the world, toward the coach. They had been off on their own.

"Worn yourselves out up in the fields?" bawled the wild young man, and he got the driver to sound the horn on the wheel insistently at them.

"You can ring from my place," said the woman.

The old man put on his air of being offended.

"You might buy my house," she tempted.

The two lovers arrived and everyone laughed. The girl —so like his wife when she was young—smiled at him.

"No. I can get the train back from Brighton," the old man said.

"Get in," called the driver.

The old man assembled seventy years of dignity. He did this because dignity seemed to make him invisible. He gave a lift to the woman's elbow, he followed her, he looked for a seat, and when she made room for him beside her, invisibly he sat there. She laughed hungrily, showing all her teeth. He gave a very wide sudden smile. The coach load chattered and some began to sing and shout and the young couple, getting into the clinch again, slept. The coach started and shook off the last of the towny places, whipped through short villages, passed pubs with animal names, The Fox, The Red Lion, The Dog and Duck, The Greyhound and one with a new sign, The Dragon. It tunneled under miles of trees, breathed afresh in scampering fields and thirty miles of greenery, public and private, until slowly, in an hour or so, the bald hills near the sea came up and, under them, distant slabs of chalk. Further and further the coach went and the bald hills grew taller and nearer.

The woman gazed disapprovingly at the young couple and was about to say something to the old man when, suddenly, at the sight of his spry profile, she began to think—in freezing panic—of criminals. A man like this was just the kind—outwardly respectable—who would go down to Hampton's garden party to case the place, as she had read, pass as a member of the staff, steal jewelry, or plan a huge burglary. Or come to her house and bash her. The people who lived only a mile and a half from where she lived had had burglars when they were away: someone had been watching the house. They believed it was someone who had heard the house was for sale. Beside her own front door, behind a bush, she kept an iron bar. She always picked it up before she got her key out—in case. She saw herself now suddenly hitting out with it passionately, so that her heart raced; then having bashed the old man, she calmed down, or rather, she sailed into one of her exalted moods. She was wearing a heavy silver ring with a large brown stone in it, a stone which looked violet in some lights, and she said in her most genteel, far-away voice, "When I was in India, an Indian prince gave this ring to me when my husband died. It is very rare. It is one of those rings they wear for protection. He loved my husband. He gave it to me. They believe in magic."

She took it off and gave it to the old man.

"I always wear it. The people down the road were burgled."

The old man looked at the ring. It was very ugly and he gave it back to her.

What fools women are, he thought, and felt a huge access of strength. But aloud he said, "Very nice." And not to be outdone, he said, "My wife died in the Azores."

She took a deep breath. The coach had broken through the hills, and now cliffs of red houses had built up on either side and the city trees and gardens grew thicker and richer. The sunlight seemed to splash down in waves between them and over them. She grasped his arm.

"I can smell the sea already!" she said. "What are you going to tell your daughter-in-law when you ring up? I told the driver to stop at the station."

"Tell them?" said the old man. A brilliant idea occurred to him.

"I'll tell them I just dropped in on the Canary Islands," he said.

The woman let go of his arm, and after one glance, choked with laughter.

"Why not?" he said, grinning. "They ask too many questions. Where have you been? What are you doing? Or I might say Boulogne. Why not?"

"Well, it's nearer," she said. "But you must explain."

The wild young man suddenly shouted, "Where's he taking us now?" as the coach turned off the main road.

"He's dropping us at the station," the woman called

out boldly. And indeed, speeding no more, grunting down side streets, the coach made for the station and stopped at the entrance to the station yard.

"Here we are," she said. "I'll get my car."

She pulled him by the sleeve to the door and he helped her out.

They stood on the pavement, surprised to see the houses and shops of the city stand still, every window looking at them. Brusquely cutting them off, the coach drove away at once downhill and left them to watch it pass out of sight. The old man blinked, staring at the last of the coach and the woman's face aged.

It was the moment to be memorable, but he was so taken aback by her heavy look that he said, "You ought to have stayed on, gone to the party."

"No," she said, shaking brightness onto the face. "I'll get my car. It was just seeing your life drive off—don't you feel that sometimes?"

"No," he said. "Not mine. Theirs." And he straightened up, looked at his watch and then down the long hill. He put out his hand.

"I'm going to have a look at the sea."

And indeed, in a pale-blue wall on this July day, the sea showed between the houses. Or perhaps it was the sky. Hard to tell which.

She said, "Wait for me. I'll drive you down. I tell you what—I'll get my car. We'll drive to my house and have a cup of tea or a drink, and then you can telephone from there and I'll bring you back in for your train."

He still hesitated.

"I dreaded that journey. You made me laugh," she said.

And that is what they did. He admired her managing arms and knees as she drove out of the city into the confusing lanes.

"It's nice of you to come. I get nervous going back,"

she said as they turned into the drive of one of the ugliest
bungalows he had ever seen, on top of the Downs, close
to a couple of ragged firs torn and bent by the wind. A
cat raced them to the door. She showed him the iron bar
she kept close to it, behind the bush. A few miles away
between a dip in the Downs was the pale-blue sea again,
shaped like her lower lip.

There were her brass Indian objects on the wall of the
sitting room; on the mantelpiece and leaning against the
mirror he had walked through was the photograph of her
husband. Pull down a few walls, reface the front, move
out the furniture, he thought, that's what you'd have to
do, when she went off to another room, and wearing a
white dress with red poppies on it, came back with the
tea tray.

"Now telephone," she said. "I'll get the number." But
she did not give him the instrument until she heard a
child answer it. That killed her last suspicion. She heard
him speak to his daughter-in-law, and when he put the
telephone down she said grandly, "I want twenty-one
thousand pounds for the house."

The sum was so preposterous that it seemed to ex-
plode in his head and made him spill his tea in his saucer.

"If I decide to sell," she said, noticing his shock.

"If anyone offers you that," he said dryly, "I advise you
to jump at it."

They regarded each other with disappointment.

"I'll show you the garden. My husband worked hard in
it," she said. "Are you a gardener?"

"Not any longer," he said as he followed her sulking
across the lawn. She was sulking too. A thin film of cloud
came over the late afternoon sky.

"Well, if you're ever interested let me know," she said.
"I'll drive you to the station."

And she did, taking him the long way round the coast
road, and there indeed was the sea, the real sea, all of it,

spread out like the skirt of some lazy old landlady with children playing all along the fringes on the beaches. He liked being with the woman in the car, but he was sad his day was ending.

"I feel better," she said. "I think I'll go to Hampton's after all," she said watching him. "I feel like a spree."

But he did not rise. Twenty-one thousand! The ideas women have! At the station he shook hands and she said, "Next time you come to Brighton . . ." and she touched his rose with her finger. The rose was drooping. He got on the train.

"Who is this lady friend who keeps ringing you up from Brighton?" his daughter-in-law asked in her lowing voice several times in the following weeks. Always questions.

"A couple I met at Frenchy's," he said on the spur of the moment.

"You didn't say you'd seen Frenchy. How is he?" his son said.

"Didn't I?" said the old man. "I might go down to see them next week. But I don't know. Frenchy's heard of a house."

But the old man knew that what he needed was not a house.

The Diver

In a side street on the Right Bank of the Seine where the river divides at the Île de la Cité, there is a yellow and red brick building shared by a firm of leather merchants. When I was twenty I worked there. The hours were long, the pay was low, and the place smelled of cigarettes and boots. I hated it. I had come to Paris to be a writer, but my money had run out and in this office I had to stick. How often I looked across the river, envying the free lives of the artists and writers on the other bank. Being English, I was the joke of the office. The sight of my fat pink innocent face and fair hair made everyone laugh; my accent was bad, for I could not pronounce a full "o"; worst of all, like a fool, I not only admitted I hadn't got a mistress, but boasted about it. To the office boys this news was extravagant. It doubled them up. It was a favorite trick of theirs, and even of the salesman, a man called Claudel with whom I had to work, to call me to the street door at lunchtime and then, if any girl or woman passed, they would give me a punch and shout, "How much to sleep with this one? Twenty? Forty? A hundred?" I put on a grin, but to tell the truth, a sheet of glass seemed to come down between me and any female I saw.

About one woman the lads did not play this game. She was a woman between thirty and forty, I suppose: Mme.

Chamson, who kept the menders and cleaners down the street. You could hear her heels as she came, half running, to see Claudel, with jackets and trousers of his on her arm. He had some arrangement with her for getting his suits cleaned and repaired on the cheap. In return—well, there was a lot of talk. She had sinfully tinted hair built up high over arching, exclaiming eyebrows, hard as varnish, and when she got near our door there was always a joke coming out of the side of her mouth. She would bounce into the office in her tight navy-blue skirt, call the boys and Claudel together, shake hands with them all, and tell them some tale which always ended, with a dirty glance around, in whispering. Then she stood back and shouted with laughter. I was never in this secret circle, and if I happened to grin she gave me a severe and offended look and marched out scowling. One day, when one of her tales was over, she called back from the door, "Standing all day in that Gallery with all those naked women, he comes home done for, finished."

The office boys squeezed each other with pleasure. She was talking about her husband who was an attendant at the Louvre, a small moist-looking fellow whom we sometimes saw with her, a man fond of fishing, whose breath smelled of white wine. Because of her arrangement with Claudel, and her stories, she was a very respected woman.

I did not like Mme. Chamson: she looked to me like some predatory bird; but I could not take my eyes off her pushing bosom and her crooked mouth. I was afraid of her tongue. She caught on quickly to the fact that I was the office joke, but when they told her that on top of this I wanted to be a writer, any curiosity she had about me was finished. "I could tell him a tale," she said. For her I didn't exist. She didn't even bother to shake hands with me.

Streets and avenues in Paris are named after writers;

there are statues to poets, novelists and dramatists, making gestures to the birds, nursemaids and children in the gardens. How was it these men had become famous? How had they begun? For myself, it was impossible to begin. I walked about packed with stories, but when I sat in cafés or in my room with a pen in my hand and a bare sheet of paper before me, I could not touch it. I seemed to swell in the head, the chest, the arms and legs, as if I were trying to heave an enormous load onto the page and could not move. The portentous moment had not yet come. And there was another reason. The longer I worked in the leather trade and talked to the office boys, the typists there and Claudel, the more I acquired a double personality: when I left the office and walked to the Métro, I practiced French to myself. In this bizarre language the stories inside me flared up, I was acting and speaking them as I walked, often in the subjunctive, but when I sat before my paper the English language closed its sullen mouth.

And what were these stories? Impossible to say. I would set off in the morning and see the gray, ill-painted buildings of the older quarters leaning together like people, their shutters thrown back, so that the open windows looked like black and empty eyes. In the mornings the bedding was thrown over the sills to air and hung out, wagging like tongues about what goes on in the night between men and women. The houses looked sunken-shouldered, exhausted, by what they told; and crowning the city, was the church of Sacré-Coeur, very white, standing like some dry Byzantine bird, to my mind hollow-eyed and without conscience, presiding over the habits of the flesh and—to judge by what I read in newspapers—its crimes also; its murders, rapes, its shootings for jealousy and robbery. As my French improved, the secrets of Paris grew worse. It amazed me that the crowds I saw on the street had survived the night and many indeed looked as sleepless as the houses.

After I had been a little more than a year in Paris—
fourteen months, in fact—a drama broke the monoto-
nous life of our office. A consignment of dressed skins
had been sent to us from Rouen. It had been sent by
barge—not the usual method in our business. The barge
was an old one and was carrying a mixed cargo, and
within a few hundred yards from our warehouse it was
rammed and sunk one misty morning by a Dutch boat
taking the wrong channel. The manager, the whole
office, especially Claudel, who saw his commission go to
the bottom, were outraged. Fortunately the barge had
gone down slowly near the bank, close to us; the water
was not too deep. A crane was brought down on another
barge to the water's edge and soon, in an exciting week,
a diver was let down to salvage what he could. Claudel
and I had to go to the quay, and if a bale of our stuff came
up, we had to get it into the warehouse and see what the
damage was.

Anything to get out of the office. For me the diver was
the hero of the week. He stood in his round helmet and
suit on a wide tray of wood hanging from four chains,
and then the motor spat, the chains rattled and down he
went with great dignity under the water. While the diver
was under water, Claudel would be reckoning his commission over again—would it be calculated only on the
sale price or on what was saved? "Five bales so far," he
would mutter fanatically. "One and a half percent." His
teeth and his eyes were agitated with changing figures.
I, in imagination, was groping in the gloom of the river-
bed with my hero. Then we'd step forward; the diver was
coming up. Claudel would hold my arm as the man appeared with a tray of sodden bales and the brown water
streaming off them. He would step off the plank onto the
barge, where the crane was installed, and look like a
swollen frog. A workman unscrewed his helmet, the visor

was raised, and then we saw the young diver's rosy, cheerful face. A workman lit a cigarette and gave it to him, and out of the helmet came a long surprising jet of smoke. There was always a crowd watching from the quay wall, and when he did this, they all smiled and many laughed. "See that?" they would say. "He is having a puff." And the diver grinned and waved to the crowd.

Our job was to grab the stuff. Claudel would check the numbers of the bales on his list. Then we saw them wheeled to our warehouse, dripping all the way, and there I had to hang up the skins on poles. It was like hanging up drowned animals—even, I thought, human beings.

On the Friday afternoon of that week, when everyone was tired and even the crowd looking down from the street wall had thinned to next to nothing, Claudel and I were still down on the quay waiting for the last load. The diver had come up. We were seeing him for the last time before the weekend. I was waiting to watch what I had not yet seen: how he got out of his suit. I walked down nearer at the quay's edge to get a good view. Claudel shouted to me to get on with the job, and as he shouted I heard a whizzing noise above my head and then felt a large, heavy slopping lump hit me on the shoulders. I turned round and, the next thing, I was flying in the air, arms outspread with wonder. Paris turned upside down. A second later, I crashed into cold darkness, water was running up my legs swallowing me. I had fallen into the river.

The wall of the quay was not high. In a couple of strokes I came up spitting mud and caught an iron ring on the quay wall. Two men pulled my hands. Everyone was laughing as I climbed out.

I stood there drenched and mud-smeared, with straw in my hair, pouring water into a puddle that came from me, getting larger and larger.

"Didn't you hear me shout?" said Claudel.

Laughing and arguing, two or three men led me to the shelter of the wall where I began to wring out my jacket and shirt and squeeze the water out of my trousers. It was a warm day, and I stood in the sun and saw my trousers steam and heard my shoes squelch.

"Give him a hot rum," someone said. Claudel was torn between looking after our few bales left on the quay and taking me across the street to a bar. But checking the numbers and muttering a few more figures to himself, he decided to enjoy the drama and go with me. He called out that we'd be back in a minute.

We got to the bar and Claudel saw to it that my arrival was a sensation. Always nagging at me in the office, he was now proud of me.

"He fell into the river. He nearly drowned. I warned him. I shouted. Didn't I?"

The one or two customers admired me. The barman brought me the rum. I could not get my hand into my pocket because it was wet.

"You pay me tomorrow," said Claudel, putting a coin on the counter.

"Drink it quickly," said the barman.

I was laughing and explaining now.

"One moment he was on dry land, the next he was flying in the air, then plonk in the water. Three elements," said Claudel.

"Only fire is missing," said the barman.

They argued about how many elements there were. A whole history of swimming feats, drowning stories, bodies found, murders in the Seine sprung up. Someone said the morgue used to be full of corpses. And then an argument started, as it sometimes did in this part of Paris, about the exact date at which the morgue was moved from the island. I joined in, but my teeth had begun to chatter.

"Another rum," the barman said.

And then I felt a hand fingering my jacket and my trousers. It was the hand of Mme. Chamson. She had been down at the quay once or twice during the week to have a word with Claudel. She had seen what had happened.

"He ought to go home and change into dry things at once," she said in a firm voice. "You ought to take him home."

"I can't do that. We've left five bales on the quay," said Claudel.

"He can't go back," said Mme. Chamson. "He's shivering."

I sneezed.

"You'll catch pneumonia," she said. And to Claudel: "You ought to have kept an eye on him. He might have drowned."

She was very stern with him.

"Where do you live?" she said to me.

I told her.

"It will take you an hour," she said.

Everyone was silent before the decisive voice of Mme. Chamson.

"Come with me to the shop," she ordered and pulled me brusquely by the arm. She led me out of the bar and said as we walked away, my boots squeaking and squelching, "That man thinks of nothing but money. Who'd pay for your funeral? Not he!"

Twice, as she got me, her prisoner, past the shops, she called out to people at their doors, "They nearly let him drown."

Three girls used to sit mending in the window of her shop and behind them was usually a man pressing clothes. But it was half past six now and the shop was closed. Everyone had gone. I was relieved. This place had disturbed me. When I first went to work for our firm

Claudel had told me he could fix me up with one of the mending girls: if we shared a room it would halve our expenses and she could cook and look after my clothes. That was what started the office joke about my not having a mistress. When we got to the shop Mme. Chamson led me down a passage, inside which was muggy with the smell of dozens of dresses and suits hanging there, into a dim parlor beyond. It looked out onto the smeared gray wall of a courtyard.

"Stay here," said Mme. Chamson, planting me by a sofa. "Don't sit on it in those wet things. Take them off."

I took off my jacket.

"No. Don't wring it. Give it to me. I'll get a towel."

I started drying my hair.

"All of them," she said.

Mme. Chamson looked shorter in her room, her hair looked duller, her eyebrows less dramatic. I had never really seen her closely. She had become a plain, domestic woman; her mouth had straightened. There was not a joke in her. Her bosom filled with management. The rumor that she was Claudel's mistress was obviously an office tale.

"I'll see what I can find for you. You can't wear these."

I waited for her to leave the room and then I took off my shirt and dried my chest, picking off the bits of straw from the river that had stuck to my skin. She came back.

"Off with your trousers, I said. Give them to me. What size are they?"

My head went into the towel. I pretended not to hear. I could not bring myself to undress before Mme. Chamson. But while I hesitated she bent down and her sharp fingernails were at my belt.

"I'll do it," I said anxiously.

Our hands touched and our fingers mixed as I unhitched my belt. Impatiently she began on my buttons, but I pushed her hands away.

She stood back, blank-faced and peremptory in her stare. It was the blankness of her face, her indifference to me, her ordinary womanliness, the touch of her practical fingers that left me without defense. She was not the ribald, coquettish, dangerous woman who came wagging her hips to our office, not one of my Paris fantasies of sex and danger. She was simply a woman. The realization of this was disastrous to me. An unbelievable change was throbbing in my body. It was uncontrollable. My eyes angrily, helplessly asked her to go away. She stood there implacably. I half turned, bending to conceal my enormity as I lowered my trousers, but as I lowered them inch by inch so the throbbing manifestation increased. I got my foot out of one leg but my shoe caught in the other. On one leg I tried to dance my other trouser leg off. The towel slipped and I glanced at her in red-faced angry appeal. My trouble was only too clear. I was stiff with terror. I was almost in tears.

The change in Mme. Chamson was quick. From busy indifference she went to anger.

"Young man," she said. "Cover yourself. How dare you. What indecency. How dare you insult me!"

"I'm sorry. I couldn't help . . ." I said.

Mme. Chamson's bosom became a bellows puffing outrage.

"What manners," she said. "I am not one of your tarts. I am a respectable woman. This is what I get for helping you. What would your parents say? If my husband were here!"

She had got my trousers in her hand. The shoe that had betrayed me now fell out of the leg to the floor.

She bent down coolly and picked it up.

"In any case," she said, and now I saw for the first time this afternoon the strange twist of her mouth return to her, as she nodded at my now concealing towel, "that is nothing to boast about."

My blush had gone. I was nearly fainting. I felt the curious, brainless stupidity that goes with the state nature had put me in. A miracle saved me. I sneezed and then sneezed again—the second time with force.

"What did I tell you!" said Mme. Chamson, passing now to angry self-congratulation. She flounced out to the passage that led to the shop, and coming back with a pair of trousers she threw them at me and, red in the face, said, "Try those. If they don't fit I don't know what you'll do. I'll get a shirt," and she went past me to the door of the room beyond saying, "You can thank your lucky stars my husband has gone fishing."

I heard her muttering as she opened drawers. She did not return. There was silence.

In the airless little salon, looking out (as if it were a cell in which I was caught) on the stained smeared gray wall of the courtyard, the silence lengthened. It began to seem that Mme. Chamson had shut herself away in her disgust and was going to have no more to do with me. I saw a chance of getting out but she had taken away my wet clothes. I pulled on the pair of trousers she had thrown; they were too long but I could tuck them in. I should look an even bigger fool if I went out in the street dressed only in these. What was Mme. Chamson doing? Was she torturing me? Fortunately my impromptu disorder had passed. I stood listening. I studied the mantelpiece, where I saw what I supposed was a photograph of Mme. Chamson as a girl in the veil of her first Communion. Presently I heard her voice. "Young man," she called harshly, "do you expect me to wait on you. Come and fetch your things."

Putting on a polite and apologetic look, I went to the inner door which led into a short passage only a yard long. She was not there.

"In here," she said curtly.

I pushed the next door open. This room was dim also,

and the first thing I saw was the end of a bed and in the corner a chair with a dark skirt on it and a stocking hanging from the arm, and on the floor a pair of shoes, one of them on its side. Then, suddenly, I saw at the end of the bed a pair of bare feet. I looked at the toes; how had they got there? And then I saw: without a stitch of clothing on her, Mme. Chamson—but could this naked body be she?—was lying on the bed, her chin propped on her hand, her lips parted as they always were when she came in on the point of laughing to the office, but now with no sound coming from them; her eyes, generally wide open, were now half closed, watching me with the stillness of some large white cat. I looked away and then I saw two other large brown eyes gazing at me, two other faces: her breasts. It was the first time in my life I had ever seen a naked woman, and it astonished me to see the rise of a haunch, the slope of her belly and the black hair like a mustache beneath it. Mme. Chamson's face was always strongly made up with some almost orange color, and it astonished me to see how white her body was from the neck down—not the white of statues, but some sallow color of white and shadow, marked at the waist by the tightness of the clothes she had taken off. I had thought of her as old, but she was not: her body was young and idle.

The sight of her transfixed me. It did not stir me. I simply stood there gaping. My heart seemed to have stopped. I wanted to rush from the room, but I could not. She was so very near. My horror must have been on my face, but she seemed not to notice that, but simply stared at me. There was a small movement of her lips and I dreaded that she was going to laugh, but she did not; slowly she closed her lips and said at last between her teeth in a voice low and mocking: "Is this the first time you have seen a woman?"

And after she said this a sad look came into her face.

I could not answer.

She lay on her back and put out her hand and smiled fully. "Well?" she said. And she moved her hips.

"I," I began, but I could not go on. All the fantasies of my walks about Paris as I practiced French rushed into my head. This was the secret of all those open windows of Paris, of the vulturelike head of Sacré-Coeur looking down on it. In a room like this, with a wardrobe in the corner and with clothes thrown on a chair, was enacted —what? Everything—but above all, to my panicking mind, the crimes I read about in the newspapers. I was desperate as her hand went out.

"You have never seen a woman before?" she said again.

I moved a little and out of reach of her hand I said fiercely, "Yes, I have." I was amazed at myself.

"Ah!" she said, and when I did not answer, she laughed. "Where was that? Who was she?"

It was her laughter, so dreaded by me, that released something in me. I said something terrible. The talk of the morgue at the bar, jumped into my head.

I said coldly, "She was dead. In London."

"Oh my God," said Mme. Chamson sitting up and pulling at the coverlet, but it was caught and she could only cover her feet.

It was her turn to be frightened. Across my brain, newspaper headlines were tapping out.

"She was murdered," I said. I hesitated. I was playing for time. Then it came out. "She was strangled."

"Oh no!" she said and she pulled the coverlet violently up with both hands, until she had got some of it to her breast.

"I saw her," I said. "On her bed."

"You *saw* her? *How* did you see her?" she said. "Where was this?"

Suddenly the story sprang out of me, it unrolled as I spoke.

It was in London, I said. In our street. The woman was a neighbor of ours, we knew her well. She used to pass our window every morning on her way up from the bank.

"She was robbed!" said Mme. Chamson. Her mouth buckled with horror.

I saw I had caught her.

"Yes," I said. "She kept a shop."

"Oh my God, my God," said Mme. Chamson looking at the door behind me, then anxiously round the room.

It was a sweet shop, I said, where we bought our papers too.

"Killed in her shop," groaned Mme. Chamson. "Where was her husband?"

"No," I said, "in her bedroom at the back. Her husband was out at work all day and this man must have been watching for him to go. Well, we knew he did. He was the laundry man. He used to go in there twice a week. She'd been carrying on with him. She was lying there with her head on one side and a scarf twisted round her neck."

Mme. Chamson dropped the coverlet and hid her face in her hands; then she lowered them and said suspiciously, "But how did *you* see her like this?"

"Well," I said, "it happened like this. My little sister had been whining after breakfast and wouldn't eat anything and Mother said, 'That kid will drive me out of my mind. Go up to Mrs. Blake's'—that was her name—'and get her a bar of chocolate, milk chocolate, no nuts, she only spits them out.' And Mother said, 'You may as well tell her we don't want any papers after Friday because we're going to Brighton. Wait, I haven't finished yet—here take this money and pay the bill. Don't forget that, you forgot last year and the papers were littering up my hall. We owe for a month' . . ."

Mme. Chamson nodded at this detail. She had forgotten she was naked. She was the shopkeeper and she

glanced again at the door as if listening for some customer to come in.

"I went up to the shop and there was no one there
when I got in . . ."

"A woman alone!" said Mme. Chamson.

"So I called 'Mrs. Blake,' but there was no answer. I
went to the inner door and called up a small flight of
stairs, 'Mrs. Blake'—Mother had been on at me as I said,
about paying the bill. So I went up."

"You went up?" said Mme. Chamson, shocked.

"I'd often been up there with Mother, once when she
was ill. We knew the family. Well—there she was. As I
said, lying on the bed, naked, strangled, dead."

Mme. Chamson gazed at me. She looked me slowly up
and down from my hair, then my face and then down my
body to my feet. I had come barefooted into the room.
And then she looked at my bare arms, until she came to
my hands. She gazed at these as if she had never seen
hands before. I rubbed them on my trousers, for she
confused me.

"Is this true?" she accused me.

"Yes," I said, "I opened the door and there . . ."

"How old were you?"

I hadn't thought of that, but I quickly decided.

"Twelve," I said.

Mme. Chamson gave a deep sigh. She had been sitting
taut, holding her breath. It was a sigh in which I could
detect just a twinge of disappointment. I felt my story
had lost its hold.

"I ran home," I said quickly, "and said to my mother,
'Someone has killed Mrs. Blake.' Mother did not believe
me. She couldn't realize it. I had to tell her again and
again. 'Go and see for yourself,' I said."

"Naturally," said Mme. Chamson. "You were only a
child."

"We rang the police," I said.

At the word "police" Mme. Chamson groaned peacefully.

"There is a woman at the laundry," she said, "who was in the hospital with eight stitches in her head. She had been struck with an iron. But that was her husband. The police did nothing. But what does my husband do? He stands in the Louvre all day. Then he goes fishing, like this evening. Anyone," she said vehemently to me, "could break in here."

She was looking through me into some imagined scene and it was a long time before she came out of it. Then she saw her own bare shoulder and, pouting, she said slowly, "Is it true you were only twelve?"

"Yes."

She studied me for a long time.

"You poor boy," she said. "Your poor mother."

And she put her hand to my arm and let her hand slide down it gently to my wrist; then she put out her other hand to my other arm and took that hand, too, as the coverlet slipped a little from her. She looked at my hands and lowered her head. Then she looked up slyly at me.

"*You* didn't do it, did you?" she said.

"No," I said indignantly, pulling back my hands, but she held on to them. My story vanished from my head.

"It is a bad memory," she said. She looked to me, once more, as she had looked when I had first come with her into her salon soaking wet—a soft, ordinary, decent woman. My blood began to throb.

"You must forget about it," she said. And then, after a long pause, she pulled me to her. I was done for, lying on the bed.

"Ah," she laughed, pulling at my trousers. "The diver's come up again. Forget. Forget."

And then there was no more laughter. Once, in the height of our struggle, I caught sight of her eyes: the pupils had disappeared and there were only the blind whites and she cried out, "Kill me. Kill me," from her twisted mouth.

Afterward we lay talking. She asked if it was true I was going to be a writer, and when I said Yes, she said, "You want talent for that. Stay where you are. It's a good firm. Claudel has been there for twelve years. And now, get up. My little husband will be back."

She got off the bed. Quickly she gave me a complete suit belonging to one of her customers, a gray one, the jacket rather tight.

"It suits you," she said. "Get a gray one next time."

I was looking at myself in a mirror when her husband came in, carrying his fishing rod and basket. He did not seem surprised. She picked up my sodden clothes and rushed angrily at him. "Look at these. Soaked. That fool Claudel let this boy fall in the river. He brought him here."

Her husband simply stared.

"And where have you been? Leaving me alone like this," she carried on. "Anyone could break in. This boy saw a woman strangled in her bed in London. She had a shop. Isn't that it? A man came in and murdered her. What d'you say to that?"

Her husband stepped back and looked with appeal at me.

"Did you catch anything?" she said to him, still accusing.

"No," said her husband.

"Well, not like me," she said, mocking me. "I caught this one."

"Will you have a drop of something?" said her husband.

"No, he won't," said Mme. Chamson. "He'd better go straight home to bed."

So we shook hands. M. Chamson let me out through

the shop door while Mme. Chamson called down the passage to me, "Bring the suit back tomorrow. It belongs to a customer."

Everything was changed for me after this. At the office I was a hero.

"Is it true that you saw a murder?" the office boys said.

And when Mme. Chamson came along and I gave her back the suit, she said, "Ah, here he is—my fish."

And then boldly: "When are you coming to collect your things?"

And then she went over to whisper to Claudel and ran out.

"You know what she said just now," said Claudel to me, looking very shrewd. "She said, 'I am afraid of that young Englishman. Have you seen his hands?' "

Our Wife

I AGREE that my wife is a noise and a nuisance, especially in a seaport and sailing place like Southampton. Even her little eyes long for trouble. People come down to sail on the weekend, clumping about in gum boots and sweaters, and they hear Molly's voice and ridicule by the quay: "Stupid yachting people! Look at *him.* He's missed the mooring twice. They can't even sail."

In the restaurant—it is called The Ship—it is ten to one she will be shouting, and then she'll suddenly stop dead. "Why does everyone stare?" she says.

"I expect it is because your conversation is more interesting than theirs," I say.

And Trevor, who is with us, of course, and who always repeats her last phrase or mine, slaps his eager knee and says, "Yes, more interesting."

"After all, you *were* talking about my first wife," I say.

Another slap from Trevor, who grins and says, "Your first wife!"

Molly is as noisy as a guttersnipe. Or as Jack (I remember) once said, "As noisy as a blowlamp, but pretty." Jack was her first husband.

The noise is what has attracted us all to her. We have loved it. She has opinions about everything. She loves an argument. Anything will do. In the old days, I remember,

she started a row about whether Jack and I were the same
height. He was, in fact, exactly the same height as myself
—six feet one and a half inches. She wouldn't have it.
About height she is a fanatic. She is under five feet high,
and one of her boasts is that her father was the shortest
captain in the Royal Navy. I can see her getting up on a
chair in the sitting room to peer at the pencil marks we
had made on the wall. Standing on the chair, she was the
same height as ourselves. This wonder silenced her, but
when I helped her down she was arguing again. Our
ruler was wrong and so was the tape measure—the taunts
shot up at us like a boy's pellets. Jack and I stood looking
like a pair of fools who had overgrown our strength,
while she went on to say that most of the weights and
measures used in shops were fraudulent.

"They probably are," Jack said.

"There you are," she jeered at me.

"Jack's right," I said.

She gaped at us. "I see," she said. "You've fixed it
between you."

Those were happy days.

That memory of Jack and me standing against the wall
ten years ago takes me to something else—what he said
in a pub in the little place on the Kent coast where they
then lived. She was sitting on a bar stool between two
men who were arguing with her about sailing—her father, the Captain, had been a tartar about boat behavior
when she was a child, and she hated sailing more than
anything—and Jack and I heard her say to one of them,
"You want cooling down," and she put her hand out for
the ice bucket. If she had been tall enough, she would
have reached it and emptied it over their heads.

Jack was ill, as he often was in those days. In the lazy,
detached, speculative voice of the very sick, he said, "See
that? Two of them. Molly is a girl who needs two husbands at a time."

He had seen something I had never noticed, and he said this with a little malice. He was either warning or defining me—or even arranging for the succession.

I am a construction engineer and I was working near their village on a new dock for tankers that was being built in this marsh country. I was a widower living in lodgings, without much to do in my spare time except play about with my boat. All those attacks on people who sailed were really attacks on me. It was one of the bonds between us—her hatred of my boat. She and Jack lived in an old house in the village that had become a hell of trucks and bulldozers on the way to the dock. I got to know Jack and Molly when a big tree was blown down in a gale in their garden and made a large gash in a brick wall. I talked to them and very soon I was offering to clear up the mess. Molly's husband was not strong enough. He was hacking at the tree with a weak man's fury, and was soon exhausted. I got a machine from the dock, and soon they were watching me work. I am a practical man. I'm good at things like that. The noise of the machine drowned her opinion of what I was doing. All she could do was to shake her brown hair.

In the following evenings, I rebuilt the wall and she stood arguing that it was "only a theory" that plumb lines hang straight. After that job was done I was captured. It was an old house, and soon I was mending doors, unstopping drains, relagging pipes, putting in washers, repairing their car. I even painted a door bright blue after she and Jack quarreled about the colors. And all the time she was arguing about how our dock would pollute the river, destroy the countryside, and drive away the bird life.

"Think of the tankers bringing oil for your car," I'd say.

Then she would turn on Jack's doctors, on hospitals, and then on Jack and me. Men were always up to something. "You can't deny it," she would say. "Look at Jack. Look at you. It's guilt."

I don't know what she meant by "guilt" and I don't think Jack did, either, but it made us feel more interesting. She'd get on to "guilt" and say Jack was oversexed, or turn about and say he was undersexed. Or that he threw money away. Or never spent a penny. Or was shut up in himself. Or perpetually running after other women. She wore her hair short and had the habit of giving a nervous sniff in the middle of her sentences— an original and wistful sound in the general clatter which attracted me—and her face would go very red while her mouth went sputtering gaily away like a little motorbike. Jack listened to her, blinking busily as if he were taking notes. After a tirade, he'd get up, give a nod, and say quietly, "She's an old character." And he would go off, leaving me with her. I would often get up to go with him, but she would stop me. "Stay here. He's going to sit on the sea wall. Leave him alone. It may be a poem."

For Jack was a poet; here was the fascination for me. In my trade I'd never run across a poet. Goodness knows how they lived—he read for publishers, I think—but every so often he would go up to his room or sit on the sea wall, and as if he were some industrious hen, he would (as I once said) lay a poem. Molly was angry with me when I said that. She allowed no one to make jokes about his poems except herself.

I wish I had not made this joke, for in a few months his health got very bad. He collapsed. It was I who took him to hospital. I thought he simply had an ulcer. He sat up in bed with a tube in his mouth and I tried to cheer him up.

"You must not make me laugh," he said. "It will tear the stitches."

In a few days he came home, walked down the village street, and took a glass of whiskey when he got back, and that night he died.

The first thing Molly said to me was indignant. "He borrowed five pounds from me this morning," she said.

Then she became exalted and tender. "It was wonderful that he left the hospital the day before that nurse who was so good to him was leaving. She couldn't bear the matron. No one could."

Then her grief overcame her. "I can't bear it," she wept. "I can't believe he isn't upstairs now."

"Neither can I," I said. "I've never felt like this before."

I loved Jack. I loved her. I had, I felt, been married to both of them.

"The lock on the wardrobe door has gone again," she suddenly said, angrily weeping and accusing me.

I put my arm round her shoulders. She had become motionless and heavy as lead with grief, and she shook my arm off.

"I'll go and look at it," I said. "Leave it to me."

For a poor man, Jack had occasional reckless fits. He hankered after expensive antiques. This wardrobe I knew well, for I had three or four times tried to repair the lock for them. Owing to the weight of the doors, it was often going wrong. The wardrobe was an oaken piece brought over from France by Huguenots—so Molly swore—in the seventeenth century and it stood in their bedroom. It was the first of Jack's purchases, and she and he had a monumental row about it. She had been going to send it back to the shop, but Jack saved it in a very clever way: he wrote a poem about it. This made it sacred in her eyes. After this, he became a secret furniture buyer and had to store the stuff out of her sight, and once or twice I collected it for him.

"So that is what you and Jack were up to," she said after he died. She admired our shadiness. To punish me —and Jack, too—she sold the lot, but not the wardrobe.

The furniture episode became another bond between us, especially because of the to-ings and fro-ings of the sale, during the time of her grief. Her grief recalled mine when my wife had died, and we often talked about it. She would gaze and nod and talk quietly. She became, except for the tiny sniff, a soundless person. Slowly her grief passed. After a year, my job at the dock came to an end. I was to be moved to the London office and I started packing.

Molly's character suddenly returned to her when she saw my clothes stacked on the table in my lodgings. "It's a good thing!" she said. "It will get you away from that idiotic boat."

My transfer to London was a victory for her opinion. She glittered with victory.

"I'll take you out in it," I said, "for a last sail."

I was astonished, even moved, by her reply. "All right!" she said defiantly, but I could see that, despite her victory, her lip was trembling. I could see that she did not want me to leave, and I didn't want to leave her. I knew that when we were out on the water and I was, perhaps, coming about and making her duck the boom, I would be able to say what I could not say to her on land. We set off, but soon it began to blow, the sails rapped out, and the wind carried away everything she said. She was indignant and frightened. When we got ashore she said, "You're a masochist, like Jack. It is all guilt."

"I'm going to sell her," I said, looking down at the boat from the quay wall. While we were out and I was putting in a reef, I had asked her to marry me.

"When you sell it," she said.

I sold it.

Unluckily for her, we hadn't been married for three months when the firm moved me from London back to Southampton. There was the sea again! There were those detested lovely white tents dotted over the water.

"All yachtsmen are liars," she said when she saw them, accusing me of arranging my transfer. I paid no attention to her; in fact, the trouble we had moving the furniture to our house took her mind off it.

Our house at Southampton was small. I wanted to put the wardrobe—she called it the "armoire"—on the ground floor, but she said it must go into the bedroom. To get it up there I had to take out a tall window and put a hoist in from an attic. The thing weighed a ton. It took two days and three men to get it into the bedroom. It had been Jack's first extravagance, and Molly was very proud of the difficulty it caused. She stood in the garden shouting at the men and came peering at it, to see they did not damage it. In fact, the lock did scrape the brickwork when the thing was halfway in.

The scrape on the brickwork must have weakened the lock, or perhaps the damp summer affected the doors in some way, for they did not easily close. In the winter, there would be a sudden click and one door would swing forward. I put it right, and then, after a malicious lull, the wardrobe—the armoire, I should say—would come open again. Sometimes I worked on the lock; sometimes I wedged and re-wedged the feet, blaming the slope of the floor.

In the end, I succeeded, and for a long time the thing was quiet. But one night when I was making love to Molly a door came groaning open like a hound.

"What's that?" said Molly, pushing me away.

I paused in my efforts. "It's only Jack," I said. "It's haunted."

Now, why on earth I should have said such an appalling thing, and at such a moment, I cannot think. If there is one thing we all know, it is that you should never make a joke—if you call that a joke—when you are making love. I would have given anything to take the words back. Perhaps it was a sign that I was beginning to want help, as Jack had done. Hadn't he said she was a woman who needed two husbands?

The effect on Molly was surprising. She sat up, put on the light, and looking excitedly at the doors she laughed. " 'Haunted'—that's very perceptive of you," she said, admiring me.

I was shocked by her laugh and pushed her down again. (But to be frank, love was a fitful thing with Molly. Now that we were married, she said I bullied her into it.) She got free of my arms, put on the light once more, gave herself a little shake like a dog, and gazed in a rapture of importance. "It's weird," she said. "It *could* be haunted. Jack always said nothing is forgotten."

Molly loved to sit up arguing in the middle of the night when I was exhausted. She said that all things were permeated by the people who had touched them. Now I made my second mistake: I said the armoire was probably alive with the hands of Huguenots. This idea annoyed her.

"It's very funny about you," she said. "I didn't know you were a jealous man. Or are you trying to change the subject?"

Jack! Huguenots! All of you! Listen to this! I want help! I cried to myself.

We were still arguing at three o'clock, when she changed round and said, "I'm glad you're not a jealous man. That means a lot to me."

I was carried away by this compliment and the softness of her voice. Only exhaustion could have put me off my guard.

Working in Southampton, I could see from my office window the sloping funnels of liners, the cranes dipping toward them and, beyond that, the water. As I have said, there was always a sail or two in sight, and on weekends there were scores of them. I had sometimes to go to the boatyards and there I would look with longing at some craft with beautiful lines on the stocks outside the sheds. The wings of the angry gulls and their quarreling voices made me think of Molly with love, and it was while I was gazing in this weak mood at a beautiful, dark-blue thirty-foot sloop one afternoon that a man climbed out of her. He was a tall, lazy-voiced fellow, with a tired face, very slim and fair.

"She's lovely," I said.

"Lovely," he said.

"Cigarette?" I said.

"Cigarette? Thanks," he said. "I am selling her."

"Selling her?" I said.

He nodded. I nodded. An interesting fellow—quiet, a listener. We walked round the boat and had a look inside.

"Frankly," he said, "I can't afford her. I've got to give her up. I've just bought an Aston-Martin. I can't run both."

Speed was what he liked, he said. He liked to *move*. He gave a lick to his lip; he was a man like myself, a man giving up one thing for another. I sighed at our singular unity.

"We might do a deal—if I can persuade my wife," I said.

"Ah," he said, "your wife."

His name was Trevor. I asked him to come up to the house later and have a drink. "But not a word," I said.

Trevor was an understanding man.

"Who is this man you're bringing up here?" my wife said when I told her. "One of your sailing friends—I know! What are you and he up to?"

"No," I said. "He's given up sailing. He can't afford it."

One more victory was in my wife's small eyes. And when Trevor arrived, wearing a white pullover under his dandyish long jacket, and very narrow trousers, she looked from one to the other of us to see who was the taller. I saw her immediate interest. Without realizing it,

I was at the beginning of a master stroke. I had brought
to the house a tall man who had given up boats. She was
excited by the arrival of an ally.

"My husband's mad about them, quite out of his
mind," she said to Trevor. "He's thinking of them all the
time. He's always up to something, hanging around
boatyards—don't think I don't know. He pretends he's
at the engineer's, but it's always a boat."

"A boat," said Trevor. There was a gentle, weary note
in his voice, and it conveyed to her that mine was one of
those infantile and tedious vices that afflict so many men
and from which he was now free.

"Better than chasing women," I said.

"Women!" she said. "It's a substitute! Don't tell me."

Trevor listened to us with appreciation as we wran-
gled. He lived alone, and he looked with pleasure at the
excitements of home life. My wife, walking up and down
and clattering on, with a glass in her hand, was adding
to her victories, and Trevor occasionally glanced at me
with private congratulation.

"I'll tell you what happened the other night!" she
cried. "We've got an old French armoire in our bedroom
and the lock keeps going wrong. He makes out he's repaired it, but I don't know—its weird! It opens every
time we get into bed. Do you know what Tom said? He
said, 'I bet that's my first wife again.' " She gave a loud
laugh. "Look at his face. Guilt."

"Guilt it must be," I said.

"You've been married before?" said Trevor—his first
original sentence. I felt gratitude to him for saying this;
it created an intimacy.

"Of course he has," said my wife. "He keeps quiet
about it. That's what is infuriating about him. He keeps
so quiet."

"Jack was quiet," I said.

"No need to bring up Jack," she said in her sacred
voice.

"Who was Jack?" said Trevor.

"He was my husband," she said, stopping with dignity. And then she turned on me. "Tell him about your wife's iron boot," she jeered.

"Iron boot!" said Trevor. He was overjoyed by her.

But she saw she had gone too far and calmed a little. "Not actually an iron boot," she said, and when she laughed her eyebrows were like a pair of wings. "Her skates. He took her roller-skating—roller-skating, my dear!—and one came off and she fell over and he got engaged. Poor Tom."

Then Trevor uttered his next original sentence to me: "Why can't you mend the lock?"

"He's always mending it—or says he is," she said. "He's useless with his hands."

"It's a French thing, very heavy, eighteenth-century," I said.

"Seventeenth," she said. "The Huguenots brought it over."

"Full of Huguenots," I said.

Trevor heard out this dispute, and then he uttered three original sentences. "My mother has got one," he said. "We had a lot of trouble with it. I got it right in the end."

I gazed at Trevor's hands. Like his voice, they were limp and tired. They were long and thin.

"I wish you'd mend ours," Molly said to him in a businesslike way. "And then we'd get some sleep." She gave me a sharp look.

"It's probably like my mother's," Trevor said. "They're all alike. I don't mind having a go. Tomorrow?"

I saw that I had found a treasure. The boat was as good as mine, if Trevor and I worked together on it. And there was more to it than the boat.

"There you are!" said Molly, sneering gaily at me at having an order obeyed as simply as that.

The following evening I found Trevor on the sofa in our sitting room with a large broken-veined bruise on his forehead. He had mended the lock, but he had moved my wedges, and just as he was testing it the door swung open and hit him on the head. Molly was mopping the wound.

I elected him at once as Molly's additional husband.

Our life—or, rather, my life—is more peaceful now. I don't mean less noisy or less of a wrangle, but simply that Trevor now bears some of the burden. He comes round most evenings and if he misses a few days she is out after him to find out what he is up to.

"He has girls in his flat," she says angrily when she comes back. "I know! Making out he stays in and listens to records. He never listens to ours!"

"He likes noise," I tell her. "He said so last time when he was here. It's company."

Trevor turns up again, and he and I say nothing about our transaction. She has been out with him in his racing car, which terrifies her, and to me she says, "It's nothing but sex. A substitute. You defend him, of course."

It is true that when he runs her up to London for the day I go sailing. When he brings her back she says, "Racing drivers are a lot of impotent morons."

I say to Trevor, "She's an old character."

"Character," says Trevor, slapping his knee at the word. Then with a sly look at me—for he likes danger as much as I do—he perhaps says, "Let's go and eat at The Ship." (It is near the mooring where I keep my secret boat).

We drive down, and at the first sight of a sail she starts about "the stinking yachtsmen." At dinner, she says, in a voice that makes everyone in the restaurant stop eating and stare at us, "Guilt, that is what it is! There is something going on between you two. Men!"

And when her voice drops for a second, she entrances both of us with that other noise, the little doglike sniff.

The Rescue

A F T E R the bad spring, the first two or three weeks of that summer turned on a sudden blaze and the pain went out of Mother's shoulder, and she let me buy the shortest mini-skirt in town. My tall brother and his taller friend George came down from Cambridge with beards like barley, and when I went out with them my golden hair seemed to flow from shop window to shop window as we walked by. The sunlight spanked like the cymbals and trumpets of a regimental band in the park, celebrating a triumph. And it *was* a time of victory in our family, especially for Mother. Why had we got a Socialist mayor at last? Why had the Council given in, after years of speeches, committee meetings, votes and letters to the papers, and agreed to turn the lake in the park into a lido? Who was behind all this but Mother? On top of this, there was the annual pageant; she ran that, too.

"You ought to take a rest," people said to her. There was always someone at the door—people rushed in to see her while she sat at the typewriter, made her lists, jumped to the telephone.

"Get on!" she would call to us. "Get on with it. Don't stop." She was short, stout and bouncing—born to rule.

This year she was putting on King Arthur and the Knights of the Round Table—nothing to do with the history of the town, but pageants were an annual holiday

for Mother. Instead of bossing the Council, she would
take a breath for a day or two, then start organizing the
past. I was to be one of Guinevere's ladies. Every day,
new bundles of plastic shields, helmets, spears, swords
and dresses were dumped in the house, so that there was
hardly room to sit down. And when my brother and
George came, they added Africa to it; thump, boom and
howls came off the records, and they larked about, dressing up in robes and swinging swords at each other.

Get on? We would have done that much faster but for
the people she brought in to help. She rarely came home
without some new adherent; her strong glasses picked
them out as she raced down the street on her short legs
or looked out of the car window. She caught people
suddenly, as a frog catches flies, and digested them without a blink. Just at our busiest time she brought home the
slowest young man in the town, a real plague called Ellis,
a boy of twenty. He worked in the library; I had often
seen him there when she sent me for books on the costumes of King Arthur's time.

"We want him for advice," Mother said. Ellis was Advice in person. Once he was in the house we could not
get rid of him; he sat among the helmets on one of the
sofas, gazing at Mother, worshiping her, and, between
long silences, uttering deep opinions that came up from
his boots. In this hot weather he wore a thick suit, a
waistcoat, and woolen socks. Having got him for advice,
Mother never listened to him. The only thing I ever
remember her saying to him was, "Why don't you take
your jacket off?" We said she'd brought him home to get
him to undress.

"Your boyfriend is in there," we'd say when she came
in with a new pile of costumes for the procession.

"Tell Ellis to count these," she'd say.

I would go up to him, shake my long hair from one
shoulder to the other and say, "For you. To count."

One evening I accidentally let out our secret joke

about him: "Count these, Lancelot."

Ellis ignored this. He lived for opinion, not for action.

The Lancelot joke had started because soon after Ellis had adopted us Mother lost the man who was going to take the part of Lancelot in the pageant. "Every year an accident," Mother said. "That is life." This year's Lancelot had been knocked off his bicycle by a dog and had broken his ankle.

"Don't worry," George said. "You've got a Lancelot here. Promote Ellis."

Mother ignored this but kept on worrying about her difficulty for days.

"Ellis for Lancelot," we kept on at her.

"Don't be malicious," Mother said, at her typewriter. "He lives alone in lodgings."

What was the real Lancelot like? Tall, I thought, with a fair beard and cool blue Cambridge eyes, like George's. But George said, "Don't be a nit. Arthur's knights were dwarfs. Bad food in the Middle Ages made everyone short."

Perhaps he was right. Our Lancelot was a stump, not more than five feet two inches high, with a low forehead and heavy arms. His habit of uttering opinions was a way of making himself seem taller. He hauled up his views from some deep mine inside him, and as they came up he stood on tiptoe and his chest swelled, and ignoring us, he unloaded them like coals for Mother alone.

Our joke did not make Ellis wince or laugh. Rather, it made him grow in importance and gaze even more profoundly at Mother, laboring at something he would sooner or later bring out, and when Mother came in and said she had found someone exactly fitted for the part, we saw Ellis looking scornfully at us and even more admiringly at Mother.

"I'm glad," he said. "If you had asked me, I would have had to refuse."

Refuse Mother! We were amazed.

"On principle," he said.

We were putting the helmets into boxes and we stopped.

"He was an adulterer," Ellis said.

We all laughed, except Mother.

"It happens to be a fact," Ellis said.

"But—" we all shouted together. We were soon at it, shouting about history, art and life, love and sex.

"Let him speak," said Mother, getting on with her work.

"It has nothing to do with history," he said. "If I had my way, I would pass a law making adultery illegal. If a man or woman committed it, they would be brought to the courts, tried, fined two hundred pounds, and imprisoned for two years."

"Why two hundred?" my brother said.

"Back to the Middle Ages," said George. "You said you're not influenced by history!"

"And when they came out of jail, I would have them branded on the back of the hand."

"With the letter *A* like in Nathaniel Hawthorne," I said. I had read him that term at school.

Ellis looked at me and for the first time smiled, congratulating me for having read the book.

"That's right," he said.

"You mean you'd make Lancelot march in the pageant wearing a letter *A* on his hand?" George said.

"Yes," said Ellis.

"You'd make it fashionable," said my brother.

"Anyone like to join the club?" said George, dancing about and waving his hands. "I've got my *A*. I see you've got yours. What about it?"

Because George did this and to show I was on his side and to make him take notice of me instead of going off with my brother all the time, I went to the desk by the window and drew a large *A* on the back of my hand.

"Look," I said, showing my hand to all of them. *"A."*

"You won't get that off in a hurry, my girl—it's marking ink," said Mother. George looked coldly at me.

The strange thing was that having uttered his thoughts and seeing us make fun of them, Ellis went flat and bewildered. He looked at Mother in appeal. He sat back on the sofa, astonished at the ruin of his ideas.

"Do you think it would make it popular?" he asked Mother simply.

Mother was holding up a red robe against George. "Is this too long for Kate Mason?" she said. "I haven't been listening." And to be kind to Ellis she changed the subject and said to him, "The mayor's opening the lido tomorrow, three o'clock. Bring your trunks."

It is strange to see adoration harden into fear. Ellis seemed to step back to the shadows of his lodgings suddenly, away from us.

"I can't get off from the library tomorrow," he said.

A simple statement, of course, but a contradiction of Mother's order. She was not used to being refused anything. She put the robe down. "I will speak to Mrs. Lowkes," Mother said. Mrs. Lowkes was the librarian, and when Mother said "speak" she meant she would require Mrs. Lowkes to do as she was told.

One shock leads to another. Ellis stood up and looked fiercely at me and obstinately at Mother. "I haven't got a suit," he said.

"There are plenty here," said Mother.

"I can't swim," said Ellis, drawing on hidden capital.

"That doesn't matter," said Mother. "We'll teach you."

Ellis moved back toward the door of the room.

"No one can teach me," he said, heaving up a load of pride into his chest. "I hate water. My father was a sailor. *He* couldn't swim. He drowned."

"How awful," I said.

He turned to me and said, "He left my mother. She died."

Until now we had never thought of Ellis as a member of a family. We hadn't even thought of him as being human, except in a general way. Seeing he had silenced us, he added information that built up the tragic distinction of his family. "Very few sailors can swim," he said. "They are fatalists."

Ellis, our fatalist!

Mother saved us. "Don't worry," she said. "There'll be a crowd there tomorrow."

But having made his stand, Ellis got even bolder with Mother. "I don't like crowds," he said. "They'll ruin the lake."

Her adorer was telling her that she was wrong—she who had fought for eight years to get the lido for the town! He was defying her and was appealing to me.

Mother was at her sewing machine. "You mustn't hate so many things, Ellis," she said.

After he left I said, "He looked as though he was going to cry."

"No. His eyes just swell up when he looks at you," my brother said.

"I'll say!" said George.

I knew that. Ellis had very large eyes and they did swell whenever he saw me come into the library. I used to make up questions about books until I made him leave his desk and say, "I'll get that book for you."

I used to have a special look that said, "You can do better than that," or "Why do you do what you are told?" And I had another, very long look that said, "I know that when you are saying things to Mother you are really saying them to me. You are frightened of me." And I would run my forefinger slowly down the edge of his desk as we talked. At sixteen, a girl likes to see what a young man will do. I hung about while other people came to the desk because I could see I was embarrassing

him. Then I went off. Once when I turned round as I got
to the door and caught him looking at me, he dropped
five books he had in his hands. There was a noise that
made everyone stare. A thrilling noise, like a tire blow-
out.

Mother got her way with the librarian, of course. Ellis
was forced to come with us to the lake. As Socialists, she
said, it was our duty to see that all mankind was happy.
We drove to the park gate, left the car, and walked the
last two hundred yards across the grass. George and my
brother ran on fast to get into the water. I raced with
them, for I liked giving Ellis a distant view of myself, and
left him and Mother dawdling behind. Ellis had the bath-
ing trunks under his arm; the bundle looked like a book
he was going to read. Presently Mother broke into a trot
to make up for lost time, talking as she ran. Ellis trotted,
too.

"I can't run in these shoes. I've ricked my shoulder,"
said Mother as she puffed up to me. She sat on a stone
bench on the stretch of concrete where the diving board
and the newly built changing rooms were. She shook her
shoulder to get her breath back, and as she gazed at the
lido she said, "Have you ever seen anything so wonderful?"

I went off and got changed. The lake was a sight! I
don't exaggerate. There were thousands of people—
well, no, hundreds—some in the water already, others
queuing up at the gate, and others lined up two deep to
get at the diving board. A flag was flying over one of the
buildings. For years the lake, which is large and with
willows hanging over the far bank, was simply ornamen-
tal and empty except for a few ducks quacking on it. Now
it was striped with bodies near the water's edge, and
farther out there were hundreds of what looked like
coconuts—the heads of the swimmers. Half the town was
there.

Ellis's first words were: "They've smashed it up." A

good description. Usually still or rippling, the water was now like a splintered mirror and there was scarcely a yard between any of the people—at any rate, not near the shore.

"A mob," Ellis said, opining.

Mother said, "Ellis, you mustn't be a snob."

Ellis heaved up a thought. "I prefer nature," he said.

"But people are nature, Ellis," Mother said.

Ellis was taken aback. He frowned. One more opinion had been ruined. His love for Mother had gone.

"Come on," said Mother to Ellis, taking off her glasses and greedy for the water. "Get your things off." And she went off to change. I had already changed, as I have said, and was made to stand guard over Ellis, who did not move. I saw he was plotting to slip away when we had gone in.

"I took a walk here last night. I often go for a walk," he said quietly to me. "It was still light. No one was about —only a dog. You could see every branch, every leaf of the trees reflected in the water, going down and down and down."

"It's only ten feet deep in the middle," I said.

"Ten feet!" he said and stepped back, wiping his fore-head with the back of his hand.

He was disappointed with me when I laughed.

There were shouts from the diving board, where a very thin man with his trunks flapping on his bones was bouncing up and down; then up went his heels. George and my brother followed him. I was longing to go. At last Mother came out, bulging in her old-fashioned black suit —an embarrassing sight. "Please get into the water quick," I wanted to say to her. But she waited to say to Ellis, "Why haven't you changed?"

Ellis gave her a lover's last pleading look and then went off miserably.

"He is scared," I said. "He thinks he'll sink through to Australia."

"Look after him and see he goes in," said Mother, who was off at once to the diving board. She went in with a thump and a man said, "Wait for the tidal wave on the other side."

I was tired of waiting, but when Ellis came out, changed, I cheated. "Good," I said and left him.

I was soon in the water. George and my brother were swimming out beyond the thick crowd along the shore. Mother was following them and I raced after them.

"Where's Ellis?" shouted Mother when I caught up.

"He's back there."

"You oughtn't to leave him like that. It's selfish."

"He can't swim."

"Teach him," Mother said. "I'll be along in a minute."

Mother was always on at me about my selfishness. So after a while I swam back and waded through the crowd.

"Good!" I shouted.

Ellis was in, all right. He was standing scarcely waist-deep in the brown water. It was strange to see only half of Ellis; it made him seem more human. People bumped into him and every time this half-Ellis was bumped he turned his head as if to say a few words. He was standing lost, as puzzled as a bust by what was going on around him. Then his arm moved; he scooped up some water in his hand and had a look at it, as if to say something about water to anyone near. But since everyone was tumbling and splashing about him, he glumly tipped the handful of water back. When he saw me, he waded back three yards to the rocky bank, with the sudden vainglory of one baptized late in life, and got out. He stood with the water pouring off his thick white body and making a pool around him. He had the furtive look of one who has done half his duty. I had done mine. I left him and went off to the diving board.

The crowd was still pouring in at the gate. The queues for the high-diving platform and the diving board were long and busy. I joined one of them and looked out for

Mother, and after a long wait I saw her. She was coming in. You couldn't miss her black suit in the crowd, and when she got to the shallow water she stood up, looking for Ellis. Then she ducked under, somersaulted and tumbled about like a kid. She was enjoying herself. Someone turned round and saw her bottom and gave it a slap. I wished she wouldn't make an exhibition of herself, but no one in the water noticed her much. They were all packed together, splashing.

I went for the high-diving platform. On my way up the crowded ladder, where people were so slow, I looked again for Mother and Ellis. I didn't see her at first, but I saw him. He was still standing on the bank, dripping, with three or four youths nearby. He was touching one or two of them on their arms, to make them listen to him. They nodded and turned away. Then he pulled at them again and started pointing. I got slowly higher up the ladder. Ellis had not got the attention of the group and his opinions were increasing. He was still pointing. Presently his shoulders straightened and his chest filled out; an enormous opinion was coming out of him—one that made them draw away, gaping shiftily at one another. And then I saw Mother. I saw her face as she rolled over on her back in the water. Her mouth was open and her face was dirty at the lips and both her legs came up in the air. Her eyes were closed. A girl next to me on the ladder said, "Look—that woman down there is in trouble. She's drowning."

Although there were several people only a yard or so away from her—two of them were actually throwing a ball over her—no one paid any attention. I pushed my way back down the ladder and then I saw Ellis turn and shout to the group that had moved back to consider her. I saw him step down in the water and wade toward her. He was alongside her, trying to get his arms round her body. She rolled out of them and then I saw mud on her feet. He was wrestling with her and calling to a man to hold her, but the man's hand slithered. Then Ellis at last got her by the slippery waist, blew out his chest, and in a struggling lunge lifted her, heaved her, blundered with her, dragging her to the bank.

I was down from the ladder and was rushing to the spot where a policeman was saying, "Put her over there," and there was Ellis alone, carrying Mother—the whole of her!—to a bench against the wall, with a trail of water following him and, after the water, a cortege of respectful people. I pushed my way among them and bumped into Ellis, who, being short, was shoved away by the crowd from the bench where Mother lay.

"She's all right," he said importantly.

Then George and my brother ran up and pushed their way into the scrum.

I can't give a clear account of what happened. I got to Mother. She looked so slimy and wet and swollen in the face. A lot of people were saying what a scandal it was— a woman drowning a few feet from the shore in a crowd like that and no one taking any notice of her; and arguments about what is nearest to the eye is hardest to see, and strong swimmers are always the weakest, and the same thing happened to a child at the town swimming bath last year, there ought to be a law, and an argument about who pulled her out. Mother came back to life quickly and the crowd thinned away, moralizing. When we got her wrapped up and sitting up, she was soon herself and very angry. I took her to the changing room and got her dressed.

"Horrible little man with his arms round me," she said. "Quite unnecessary."

"It was Ellis."

"No, it wasn't," Mother said. She'd been pulled out by some brute who tore the shoulder strap of her suit, she said. We got the car round and put her into it. Ellis was alone and stood ashamed, at a distance. He conveyed that he had not intended to intrude in a family matter.

"Come on, Ellis," my brother called.

Ellis did not answer; he looked crushed. What he wanted to do was to stand there and give a full account of what had passed while he stood arguing with the youths at the water's edge. We pushed him into the car, and Mother said irritably as we drove off, "Ellis, why don't you take off your waistcoat?"

She glowered, and when we got home and gave her a drink she went on glowering. She hated anyone to take charge of her and she hated our few cautious jokes. "My shoulder went and I lost my balance," she said. She was firm that whoever interfered and brought her in was not Ellis. He had the tact to say nothing and we were obliged to thank him with our glances.

But slowly, as we began to think back on the incident we came round, as always, in self-defense, to Mother's point of view. We stopped murmuring thanks to Ellis; it was not quite right that an outsider should rescue Mother. And there was a change in him. He had lost his habit of gazing at Mother and all desire to have an opinion seemed to have gone out of him. Before long, we were relieved to hear him say he must go. We didn't want him there all night. I went with him to the door.

"See you soon," I said, putting out my hand.

He took my hand and held it hard. His hand was not like George's or my brother's.

"Three feet of water," he said. "Three feet of water. Muddy at the bottom." Not in self-disparagement, not an opinion, though perhaps a criticism of something.

Whatever it was, we both gave a shout of laughter and shut the door, and I walked to the gate with him laughing, and the laughter so shook me from head to toe that I suddenly kissed him in a "Now-what-do-you-think-of-that?" way. All he said was, "Come out."

"I'll walk with you to the corner."

We marched down the street, silent as soldiers. We said nothing and we could hear only the sound of our shoes. It was as if our feet were talking. At the corner, where the main road begins, cars were rushing by.

"Come on," he said. And again his hand gripped mine and all the houses I knew in that street began to look different. We walked on and suddenly Ellis gave a peculiar jump, like a frog, and we laughed to the next turning and the next, from street to street, bumping together.

"Where are we going?"

"To the park."

"It's closed."

"I know a place where you can get in."

And so we did get in. The everyday smell of the pavements went and we stood in the night glow of the grass, under the trees, which were as black as men against the town lights. The sky was like pink water above us and we were sinking, sinking, sinking. My heart thumping for breath, at the bottom of the world, until somewhere near the trees Ellis stopped his little jumps and I sat down exhausted. I was clutching at him, pulling him under with me and struggling with the kisses that came out of him and throwing my hair back to get more. He looked wicked in the dark.

The next day, to the *bang, bang, bang* of the band, we marched in the pageant. It banged the way my heart banged in the park. I wore a high conical hat with a veil hanging from it. Ellis had a green jerkin and carried a pikestaff. I could hardly bear to look at him for fear of laughing, but when we got near the town hall and the band stopped, I said, "Well, Lancelot, show me the back of your hand."

"It's not the same thing," said Ellis and started to explain, but I stopped him.

I taught him to swim that summer.

About the Author

V. S. PRITCHETT was born in England in 1900. He is a short-story writer, novelist, critic and traveler. His short stories have appeared in collections in the United States under the titles *The Sailor and the Saint, When My Girl Comes Home, Blind Love* and as individual contributions in *The New Yorker* and *Holiday*. Among his novels are *Mr. Beluncle, Dead Man Leading* and *The Key to My Heart*. Random House has also published *The Living Novel and Later Appreciations*, a collection of critical essays, most of which appeared originally in *The New Statesman*, and his Clark Lectures, *Meredith and English Comedy*. He has been a lifelong contributor to this paper and is now a director. His memoirs, *A Cab at the Door* and *Midnight Oil*, were published by Random House in 1968 and 1972. In 1973 he published a life of Balzac.

Mr. Pritchett's extensive sojourns in Europe, the Middle East, and South America have led to the writing of several books on travel, among them, recently, *The Offensive Traveller*. With photographs by Evelyn Hofer, Mr. Pritchett has written *London Perceived, Dublin: A Portrait* and *New York Proclaimed*.

Mr. Pritchett has visited the United States, where he gave the Christian Gauss Lectures at Princeton, was Beckman Professor at the University of California in Berkeley, and has been writer in residence at Smith College, and Zisskind Professor at Brandeis University. He is a foreign Honorary Member of the American Academy of Arts and Letters and the American Academy of Arts and Sciences.